SHE'S ON TOP

SHE'S ON TOP

EROTIC STORIES OF FEMALE DOMINANCE
AND MALE SUBMISSION

<small>EDITED BY</small>
RACHEL KRAMER BUSSEL

CLEIS
PRESS

Published in the United States by Cleis Press Inc., P.O. Box 14697, San Francisco, California 94114.

Printed in the United States.
Cover design: Scott Idleman
Cover photograph: Celesta Danger
Text design: Frank Wiedemann
Cleis Press logo art: Juana Alicia
First Edition.
10 9 8 7 6 5 4 3 2 1

"His Just Rewards" by Rachel Kramer Bussel was originally published in *Naughty Stories from A to Z, Volume 4*, edited by Alison Tyler (Pretty Things Press, 2006). "City Lights" by Kathleen Bradean was originally published at Erotica Readers & Writers Association (www.erotica-readers.com) in February 2005.

Contents

INTRODUCTION: THE PERFECT POWER TRIP

The image of a strong, powerful woman hovering over a cowering man is enough to stop us in our tracks. Turning the tables on traditional gender roles, women who seize control over their adoring male subjects claim a power that threatens to knock us all down a notch. When a woman gets on top, whether literally or figuratively, she exudes an alluring confidence, an Amazonian stature that can make even the fiercest of men long to submit. Getting a man to willingly cede control and offer his body up to her becomes her goal, and she will do anything to get it. He, by contrast, is grateful for the chance to shed some of the macho mask he must wear day in and day out, to snivel and quake and proffer himself to her, whether to earn praise and a pat on the head or a powerful spanking or heavenly beating. He wants her to tie him up, shove her breasts in his face, and tease his cock until he's ready to explode. He longs to kneel at her feet, lick her boots, and worship her in every sense of the word, but he keeps quiet; *she* will decide when and how she wants to have her way with him.

I know from my own experiences that male submission can be a beautiful thing. It can suffuse the woman in charge with the kind of power that she can only experience within this ritualistic dynamic—power freely given, all to her. It's extravaluable because, in their daily lives, these women may not have all that much actual power, but can play with it and feel the thrill of overtaking a man in such an all-consuming way. The women of *She's on Top* don't take their power trips lightly. They know exactly what they're doing, taking the gift of their male followers and turning it into something overwhelmingly erotic. Whether it's the temp who puts her boss in his place in Donna George Storey's "Suit and Tie" or the "firm hand" employed by Debra Hyde's protagonist, there's a wink-wink quality to their naughty play. In MinaRose's "Waiting for Me," the vision of the protagonist's docile husband clamoring to be punished is enough to get her through the day. Kate Dominic summons up her character's regal poise as she sits in "The Queening Chair" and gets serviced by three men while her husband listens in.

The way these authors describe their characters' dominance demonstrates the many reasons that women enter into such relationships. Sometimes they don't even realize quite how much pleasure they derive from their position, perhaps having been conditioned to think that dominance doesn't belong in their most intimate encounters. What Saskia Walker calls "The Inner Vixen" can feel like a calling, a special pleasure these women are predestined to enjoy, once they get around to figuring out their true desire. Kristina Wright's professional dominatrix "meets her match" in a man who bares his body to give her the high she can only get from topping, one she thought she'd left at the dungeon but that has become a part of her very soul. In Teresa Noelle Roberts's bittersweet "Mark of Ownership," a cutting is a symbolic and deeply felt ritual between two lovers about to part, one in which each derives so much more than an erotic thrill. Their entire dynamic feeds off her control over him, which she exerts in a final gift of mercy by setting him free. Pushing men right up to and sometimes beyond their limits, testing and tormenting them, having the satisfaction of knowing what they want before even they do—are all the tasks of a good domme. For Caroline, the mistress in N. T. Morley's "Room 2201," this means directing a bisexual encounter that's as much for her pleasure as it is her virginal male sub's. And in Lisabet Sarai's "Shades of Red," a young visitor to Amsterdam makes good use of the city's red-light district to test out her whip hand, and see just how brave she is when it comes to realizing her kinky fantasy.

Another role of a good top is to be prepared, setting the stage for a scene that they're both desperate to play out, even though both players may know it's a game. The wife in Andrea Dale's "Working Late" doesn't want her husband to get fired, but if he thinks he might be breaking the rules, it adds a rush to his on-demand office wanking. The reverence these dommes show for their underlings lets you know just how much love and affection they share while enacting these kinky scenes. "Oh, is he sweet. He is my angel. My lover. My sweet young thing in a floral dress and tie-up espadrilles, so ready and willing to get fucked against some back-alley wall," writes Alison Tyler in "Why Can't I Be You?" Her narrator demonstrates perfectly what the real meaning of penis envy is, and the rewards are great for her and her lover as they trade places for one night.

She's on Top, along with its companion volume, *He's on Top*, is not about seizing power by any means necessary. It's about the erotic dance between top and bottom, between one who gets off on controlling another and one whose greatest fantasy is to give it up to a powerful other. The look of awe and adoration in a sub's eyes as he gazes up at his mistress, "like a devotee," in

Walker's words, ready to do whatever is asked—or ordered—of him, can provoke a high like no other. The beauty of that interplay shines from these pages, in which you'll find demanding mistresses, powerful wives, first-time dominants feeling out their newfound roles, and other bitch goddesses who reign supreme over their dominions. These women not only enjoy the ultimate of power trips; they also give their men, like the lucky fiancé in "Victoria's Hand," exactly what they most desire.

Whether you're a woman who already wields the whip (or the paddle or hairbrush or wooden spoon) in your household, a man who caters to a beautiful domme's every wish, or someone who simply gets off on seeing a woman step out of her frilly femininity to claim womanpower of another kind, you're in for a treat with this kinky, edgy, daring collection. Make that eighteen of them—and make sure you pay homage to the woman on top in your life when you're done.

Rachel Kramer Bussel
New York City
August 2006

SUIT AND TIE

Donna George Storey

The Year of the Suits. That's what I call it now, the nine months I spent working as a temp in the Financial District. I have a permanent life now—I'm living with a great guy and finishing up my master's in physical therapy—but sometimes when I'm downtown on a weekday I get a hit of those strange times.

It was bad enough dealing with the crazy bosses who acted as if the world was going to end because the caterers didn't send enough aioli for the clients' lunch buffet or we didn't get the presentation folders ready in time for the Fed Ex pickup. More deadly was the boredom, the hours I spent on hold for the travel agent who handled the company's account or tending a chugging copy machine. I probably would have gone crazy myself if I hadn't slipped into the restroom now and then to masturbate. At least it brought some excitement to the day.

What I remember best, though, was walking down the bustling streets at noon, engulfed in a wave of men in business suits. Their heads always looked blurred and faded, as if they'd been rubbed out with an eraser. It was the suits that seemed to take command as they marched purposefully toward some unknown battle of commerce. But at least once on every block, one man's face would suddenly shift into focus, and his eyes would leap out at me with such longing that my pulse would falter. I suppose it might have been mere lust for any passing flesh that was young and female. This gaze felt different, though, as if the man in question were sending a coded message from deep inside his woolen prison—*Hey, I'm alive in here.*

The weirdest thing was that I felt the urge to help the poor guy. In my daydreams, I did. I reached out and pulled away his stiff wrapper like the peel of a fruit and pressed my fingers to his warm, secret core as I whispered—*Yes, I see you.*

Of course, in the next instant, my momentary soul mate would be swept along in the tide of blue and charcoal gray, but I let myself believe that something important had happened between us. It made my own prison sentence go faster.

I never imagined that by the end of my Year of the Suits, my dream would actually come true.

It was ironic that Steve Kennedy was the man I finally did penetrate, among other X-rated activities we enjoyed in his plush office suite overlooking Montgomery Street. As bosses go, he was one of the best. It was just the two of us, with me sitting watch at the receptionist's desk. Most of the time he left me alone to email my friends, surf the Net, and race through the day's novel, which I usually finished on the commute home. Plus, he always brought *me* coffee when he popped down to the café on the corner, and he always got it right: nonfat low-foam double latte.

Now that's a good boss.

I'd guess he was in his mid-forties, but he had a pretty good

body from lunchtime workouts at the health club. His face reminded me enough of the president of the same last name that I
was sure they were distant relations. But Steve didn't have JFK's
legendary charm. He was shy, as you might expect of a tax accountant, although he was clearly bringing in the bucks. I sensed,
though, that the constraint went deeper, that he was somehow
shackled inside, even more than the typical suit rushing along
the sidewalk at lunchtime. Of course, maybe I had it wrong and
he'd found his heart's desire in a smooth, reliable life. Except
if that's really how he wanted things to go, during the weeks I
worked for him, Steve made three serious mistakes.

The first thing he did wrong was to catch me playing with
myself in the co-ed restroom in the suite. Okay, so I didn't lock
the door, but he'd just left for the health club and I wasn't expecting any clients for quite some time. He didn't even knock
either, he just pushed the door open and there I was, standing
in front of the mirror by the sink, my slacks and panties pushed
down around my thighs, my blouse open, and my hands doing the usual coffee-break-quickie cha-cha with my clit and my
nipples.

I let out a cry and covered myself as best I could. Without a
word, he stepped straight back through the door, like a movie
playing in reverse. He'd seen me, no question about that.

My heart was pounding as I straightened my clothes and
dabbed my sweaty face with a wet paper towel. I was in big
trouble. How could it be otherwise? Steve would fire me and tell
the agency, and they'd fire me and everyone in the city would
know I jerked off in the restroom during my breaks and I'd never find another job and I'd starve and...

The face in the mirror broke into a giggle.

If word got out about my activities, I'd probably get even
more work. And, really, if he did kick my ass out on the street,

he'd be doing me a favor. I might finally have to get myself a real life.

Still, the prospect of facing him after our little encounter was too daunting, even in my new *what-the-fuck?* mood, so I slipped down to the bar at the end of the block and drank two vodka martinis.

When I stumbled back into the office, he opened his door and asked to speak with me for a moment. It was pretty obvious he'd been waiting for me.

He motioned for me to sit down on the sofa and perched himself on the edge of his desk—a good choice to project benevolent authority, which seemed to be the way he'd decided to spin it. He was blushing, though, as he told me in a kind, measured voice that it wasn't his business what I did during my breaks, but he hoped in the future that I would keep the door locked in case a client wandered in.

If I hadn't had those drinks, I probably would have finished up the remaining weeks of the assignment in dutiful gratitude for his broadmindedness toward female sexual expression. However, the public, responsible me had receded to a little room in my head where it was trying its best to keep my body from slumping sideways on the sofa. That left the secret me—the honest me—to do the talking.

"Thanks," I said with a touch of insolence. "That's very cool of you to be so understanding of your employees' needs."

It was then he made his next mistake, an attempt to joke with me. "Yes, well, maybe you'd better tell your boyfriend to be more attentive to those needs."

"I don't happen to have a 'boyfriend' right now," I shot back. It was the silly high school word that bothered me, because I did have a couple of fuck buddies handy for when the urge struck, but of course, good old Steve misunderstood.

"I'm sure that's only temporary," he said gallantly.

"Temporary. Yes, well, that's me. And don't worry, I'll, um, be more careful in the future." But as I headed for the door, I carelessly staggered into him. It wasn't on purpose, exactly, but I didn't pull away when he caught my arm.

"Megan, are you okay?"

I stared at his hand resting on my bare flesh. It was a warm, sturdy hand and I couldn't help imagining his fingers at work where mine had been earlier that day. I glanced up at his lips, which looked much softer and fuller up close. My eyes dropped lower—and I'm not sure if this counts as another one of his mistakes—but you couldn't miss that tent pole poking up under the trousers.

Cut the concerned authority figure crap, Steve. You want it as much as I do, so why don't we just go ahead and fuck right here?

I didn't actually say that out loud, or maybe I did, because suddenly we were kissing and I was running my hands all over that fine gray suit. I'd been right all along, there really *was* a living body inside, warm and soft in some places, hard in others. And that body did have secret hungers—in this case, to perform a variety of adults-only activities with mine. Steve guided me back to the sofa, peeled off my pants, and asked me, with beguiling urgency, if he could eat my pussy and help finish the job he'd so rudely interrupted.

"Sure, why the hell not?" I answered, lounging back and spreading my legs. I did have an unresolved ache down there. And, after all, who could turn down such an offer?

Steve made sure to lock the door, but then he dove right in without any preliminaries, still wearing his jacket and tie. He was pretty good with his tongue, but the best part was watching him kneeling between my legs, face buried between my thighs, lips moving as if in prayer. Which is exactly what I'd dreamed about day after day on my lunchtime walks.

I was getting pretty hot from his attentions, so I asked him—more like ordered him, really—to play with my tits, too. Not long afterward, I finally did reach the climax he'd snatched from me two hours earlier. As he pulled away, he unconsciously fished one of my hairs out of his mouth, which could have been an awkward moment, but we both laughed.

"I don't mind returning the favor," I said.

"Well, I would like to make love to you, but I'm afraid I don't have any protection," he said, not quite meeting my eyes.

"Make love?" "Protection?" Was this guy quaint, or what? But by that time I was curious to see what he had in his pants, so I confessed that I carried condoms in my purse.

As he started to undress, my heart sank. Not that his body wasn't fit—I'd guessed right about the benefits of the health club—but somehow I missed the suit. Apparently I wasn't quite ready for the "uncovering his warm, secret core" part of my fantasy.

So I knelt on the carpet, stuck out my ass, and told him to take me doggy-style. Then I closed my eyes and imagined he was still fully dressed with just his red cock poking out of his fly, and his nice trousers were getting all stained with my pussy juice. This, along with the thrusting of his cock against my sensitive, post-come sweet spot, almost brought me to a second orgasm. Almost, but not quite.

Still, I left work that day in a much better mood. Yes, he'd caught me masturbating. I, however, had good evidence he'd cheated on his wife. Or maybe she was a girlfriend, but I'd taken note of the picture of a handsome, assured-looking blonde smiling out from the bookshelf behind his desk. Steve would surely realize that he and I were equals in crime and treat me accordingly.

That was my mistake.

The next morning he called me into his office as soon as I arrived. This time his blush was deeper. With much throat clearing he told me he'd enjoyed the day before, but he wasn't in a position to be pursuing a relationship right now. He hoped I would stay until the end of my assignment, but he'd understand if I didn't feel comfortable...

I wasn't the least bit drunk, but the honest me immediately took exception to his terms. "Hey, all we did was fuck on the carpet in front of your desk," I interrupted. "That's not a relationship. It's a way to make a boring afternoon go a little faster."

His head snapped back. He clearly hadn't planned for this response from docile little me. But I was suddenly tired to death of that charade.

"Too bad I spent a good ten minutes in the shower this morning shaving so I could sit on your desk and have you lick my smooth, pink twat without any worries about stray short-and-curlies in your teeth."

I pulled up my skirt to show him my slit. He stared, eyes wide.

"Listen, I like this job, so I'm staying. I'll be sitting out there with my shaved pussy all day, so if you're interested in taking care of my needs, the job's yours. But please, oh, please, don't ever think I'm expecting a relationship." I spit out the last word with a sneer and headed for the door.

It was then he made his third mistake, in a voice so low, I could barely hear it.

"Megan," he said. "Wait."

So, just as I'd imagined in the shower that morning, Steve did lift me onto his desk, and pull my skirt up to my waist, and glide my green satin panties over my legs. Then, licking his lips, he started to take off his jacket.

"Stop," I said.

He looked at me, confused.

"Don't take off your clothes. I really get off on watching a guy in a business suit eat me."

His eyes twinkled. "Whatever you say, uh, *boss*."

The oral sex was even better the second time, and I came with shuddering gasps, knocking pens and paper clips all over the floor. There were some wet spots on his tie, but he didn't seem to care. He did ask, politely, to borrow another one of my condoms, but his faintly taunting use of the word *boss* still stung a little.

"I think you should buy your own, don't you?" I jumped off the desk and smoothed my skirt. "So, you know, just give me a buzz when you're, um, protected."

I winked and walked out the door, leaving my panties behind.

Steve got the condoms at lunch, a twelve pack, but I made him eat me again before I let him fuck me. It's funny how quickly we settled into our roles. He seemed to like it when I bossed him around and made him "earn" his orgasm. Once, I ordered him to lick his lunch from my body—cucumber and tomato slices from my breasts and hummus from my shaven mons. Another time I told him I wanted him to make me come just by tonguing my asshole. It took a long time, but with some auxiliary clit action on his part, he finally got his work done.

I sucked him just once, when he was on the phone with a client, and as a reward for keeping his voice normal, I stuck my finger up his ass and did the little come-hither wiggle until he shot in my mouth with a soft groan. Most of the time I made him keep all his clothes on, and I'm sure he had lots of extra dry cleaning bills, but he never complained.

I know why *I* liked it—it was fun to be a spoiled bitch who pushed the limits and made the rules for a change—but I wondered about him. Was it a sort of Oval Office approach to infidelity? Meaning, if it's not intercourse, it's not sex? And if I don't come, it's not sex? Except Steve and I were having intercourse and he was coming, so maybe for him it was more like, if she orders me to do it, it's not sex? Or, who knows, maybe I really was nourishing something starved and withered inside him.

Eventually, however, we came up against an insurmountable limit to doing it in his office: carpet burns. I'd spent the lunch break riding him on the floor—me naked, him with his trousers pushed just halfway down his thighs. Afterward I stroked the angry red marks on my knees and said, "Wouldn't it be nice to do this on a bed?"

Again he misunderstood, as he always seemed to do when we actually talked. "I'm sorry. I believe I mentioned back at the beginning I can't take you to my place."

I snorted. "Would you stop it, already? I meant a hotel. With a big, soft, four-poster bed so I can tie you up and have my way with you."

He smiled. "You're already having your way with me."

"I think I can do much better. In the right environment."

He definitely looked intrigued. "Okay, how about tomorrow afternoon? You bring an overnight bag to throw them off when we check in."

"Good plan. But I want you to bring something for me, too."

He arched an eyebrow.

I pulled my purse over and fished out a crumpled business card for a sex toy store on Polk Street. "I want you to buy a few things from this place for me to use on you. Bring them in your briefcase. I'm not talking chocolate body paint, either. I mean the hard stuff—leather and silicone. And don't forget, if the selection isn't interesting, I won't be happy with your work."

Steve laughed uncomfortably, but I had no doubt he'd do it. He knew who was in charge.

The first thing I did when we got to our anonymous hotel room with the four-poster bed was order Steve to open his briefcase. Mixed in with folders, a calculator, and random disks and pens were a few more unusual items that he laid out on the bed precisely in ascending order of provocativeness: a blindfold, Velcro handcuffs and tethers, a narrow leather paddle, and a curved purple butt plug.

I was, frankly, surprised and impressed. And a little scared, too. I was comfortable with giving orders, but props took it to a whole new level.

"Well, it looks like we have a lot of work to do this afternoon. Why don't you get undressed?"

"You want me to take all my clothes off?" he asked warily.

"Different place, different rules. Go ahead, give me a little stockbroker's strip tease."

He smiled wryly, but his face was flushed with embarrassment.

I sat on the bed and watched as Steve took off his jacket and draped it over the chair. Next came the tie and shirt, then the trousers. He kept his eyes fixed on some spot on the carpet the whole time, submissive rather than seductive, but by the time he was done his cheeks were bright red and he had quite a bulge in his boxers.

"Take off the underwear, too. I want to watch you touch yourself. You know, just so we're even."

He began to caress his hard-on rather self-consciously. In the meantime, I pulled off my own clothes, leaving them in a pile, then walked over and snatched his jacket from the chair.

It was still warm when I slipped it on. And it was like armor, stiff and boxy, but oddly sensual, too. The faint smell of male sweat made me dizzy, and I soon discovered that every time I moved, the lapels chafed my nipples, sending shivery jolts of pleasure to my cunt.

I handed him his tie. "I want to wear this, too, and I'd like you to knot it for me."

A quick smile played over his lips, but he complied. Halfway through the attempt, he tilted his head and frowned. "May I try this in front of the mirror? I'm not used to doing it for someone else."

We stood in front of the dresser, Steve behind me.

"Would you like it snug or loose?"

"Fairly tight," I said, thinking the constriction might be a turn-on, but I regretted it. It was more like a slave collar, which might be the simplest explanation as to why those legions of businessmen looked so unhappy.

When he was done, we both studied my costume in the mirror. The shoulders of the jacket were all out of proportion, and the sleeves hung to the middle knuckles of my fingers. Plus, the tie hanging between my breasts made it all the more obvious that I was naked underneath, and the friction of the wool on my nipples was really getting distracting. Far from appropriating the symbols of male power, I looked like exactly what I was—a girl playing dress-up.

Steve seemed to think so, too. His face, hovering over my shoulder in the mirror, showed an indulgent, almost tender smile.

Fortunately, even a "cute" dominatrix could regain the upper hand when she shackled her slave in handcuffs and tethered him to the bed. When I tied his knees together with my pantyhose, he was no longer smiling, and his cock was standing at respectful attention.

"I think we're ready to get started on today's project." I

straddled him and began to rub my swollen pussy against the coarse hairs of his belly. "We'll skip the blindfold today because I want you to be able to watch what's going on. I'm not sure about the paddle. You've been such a good boy buying all these very naughty toys, I don't think you need a spanking today."

Did I detect disappointment in his face? Well, I was running the show and I had other things on the agenda, things I'd been thinking about long before I met him.

"I'm going to tell you something I've learned about your jacket. He seems to have a mind of his own," I said in a low voice. "He's rubbing up against my breasts and making me wet. But maybe that part's not such a secret?" Indeed, I'm sure we could both hear the soft smacking sounds of my arousal as I skated over him. "But he's getting a little rough with my poor nipples, and I know it would feel so good to soothe them in a warm, soft mouth. Too bad you're all tied up and can't manage it right now."

Steve stared as I opened the jacket. The nipples did look red and sore, as if they'd been bitten.

"And my poor cunt, it's so hungry and there's a hard, thick cock that's so close I can feel it knocking up against my ass, but I can't sit on it because it's not protected."

Steve sighed, arching up against me. "If this is how you planned to torture me, it's working."

I looked down at him, smiling sweetly. "Maybe that little purple cock over there will please the client? We must always do our best to please the client." I got up on my knees and buried the obscene tool in my vagina. I fucked myself with it for a few strokes, then held the glistening object in front of his face. "Oh, I forgot, this is supposed to go in someone's butt. How about yours? I know how much you like having something up your ass when you shoot."

Steve flinched, but he didn't deny it.

"Lift your legs," I ordered, and this he could do, even though they were lashed together above the knee. I tickled his opening with the tip of the plug for a while until he whimpered and his hole beckoned in invitation. "In she goes," I said, gently pushing it in to its full length.

His body tensed, then he melted back onto the bed with a sigh.

"You're being such a good boy, I think I might put Mr. Dick in his raincoat now. Because if you perform well on this next part, you'll definitely deserve a reward."

I straddled his belly again. He gazed into my face, his eyes glowing with something like fear, except it was somehow sweeter, softer.

"Steve," I said, "you've got it all wrong. I'm not doing this to torture you. I don't even like seeing you tied up like this. I want you to be free. Can you try to get free for me?"

At first he looked confused, but then seemed to understand it was part of my game.

"Try," I said softly. "When you're free you can do anything you want. You can suck my nipples and fuck me and come inside my hot, hungry cunt."

Taking his cue, Steve obediently pulled on the tethers and tensed his legs. The effort made his whole body shake, like a big vibrator between my thighs. It was another unexpected benefit for me.

"I can't do it," he said.

"Try," I urged. "I like it when you try."

He struggled against his bonds again and grunted, whether with arousal or exertion, I wasn't sure. After a few more times, I was skidding all over his belly on my juices as I rode him like a bucking horse. With our shouts and cries and the screaming bedsprings, we probably were as noisy as a rodeo. Finally I took advantage of one of his earnest, but futile, attempts at release to settle myself on the saddle of his cock.

He gasped, a low, velvet sound of longing fulfilled.

"Fuck me. Come inside me," I said, riding him in a different way now.

It was a redundant command if there ever was one, because that's what he was doing, thrusting up into me with bellowing groans. He'd never made those sounds before—in the office, he was as quiet as a mouse. This time he came with a yell so raw and shattering, it did sound as if something inside him was breaking free.

After I untied him, he took me in his arms and squeezed me so hard it hurt.

"That was good, Megan," he whispered. "So good. Thank you."

Suddenly I was aware of the choking grip of his tie, still wrapped around my neck. I reached between us and pulled it off. But even then, the tightness still lingered in my throat.

I barely recognized my shy tax accountant at work the next day. He actually bounced off to get our lattes, announcing with a wink that he didn't have any clients that afternoon.

I gave him a big smile in return, but once he was gone, I buried my face in my hands. Our offsite meeting had been a success, but I was worried about the troubling twist my thoughts had taken since. You'd think tying a guy to a bed and shoving a butt plug in his backside would lead to grander dreams of crops and strap-ons and studded corsets. But my wayward mind was intent on probing darker and more dangerous taboos—holding his hand in public, long talks about our feelings, Sunday mornings curled up together with scones and the paper. In short, a real relationship.

I felt like one sick pervert. Not to mention a liar.

Just then the phone rang and I answered, half-hoping it would be a request for Steve's more public services this afternoon so I'd have time to pull myself together.

"Hello, Cynthia?" It was a woman's voice.

"Cynthia's on maternity leave until the end of the month. I'm Megan."

"Oh, yes, that's right." The woman actually sniffed. "Well, Megan, I've been trying to get in touch with Steve all morning but he must have turned his cell phone off. Is he there?"

"No, he stepped out for a moment."

"Damn him, just when I really needed to get a hold of him. Well, could you please tell him we finished the project early and I'll be home Friday. He should call me as soon as he gets back."

She hung up before I could reply.

Here was a woman who was clearly used to being obeyed.

I allowed myself one brief moment to smile.

Then I quickly gathered my things from the desk drawers—it wasn't much—grabbed the call memo pad, and wrote out my last order to him: "Call your wife."

I had a good ten minutes to make my get-away before Steve came back. The alternative—the guilty apologies, the assurances he did care for me in his own way, the bittersweet good-bye sex on his desk—was all just too dreary.

I knew it would be best for both of us to tie it up with the girl disappearing into thin air, leaving a faint, sweet soreness in his wrists and ass to remind him she really did exist once, even if she was only temporary.

I never saw him again, so I don't know if he was totally on board with that. But it was obvious I had to be the one to come up with our strategic approach and execute the plan.

After all, I was the boss.

BY A FIRM HAND

Debra Hyde

Lounging on the deck, book in hand, cool in her sundress in the early evening shade, Judith relaxed. Surrounded by the evening cacophony of nearby birdsong and the hard *ping* of a more distant aluminum bat, she mused that these were the sounds of suburbia on an early summer evening. Yet the squabble of robins in the next yard and the cheers of the crowd on the sports field two blocks away weren't the sounds she was keen to hear. The sounds she lusted after came from inside the house—from the kitchen, to be specific—and she waited for them to carry through the open kitchen window.

The reward came in the form of clanging pots and pans. Robert was finally getting to the scrubbing part of his punishment.

Serves him right, she thought. *That'll teach him.*

It wasn't his masturbation that she was punishing. No, not at all. Judith understood the male drive and its neediness and how the convergence of such things would result in a man's taking his dick in hand. She accepted how orgasm brings relief. What Judith couldn't tolerate was Robert's messiness and, even worse, his lack of respect for her possessions. That he left his dirty magazines lying about—on their marital bed, no less!—irked her, but what really raised her ire was the pair of soiled panties she'd found there.

They were emerald green, soft and silky, and had cost her good money. She had found them amid the mess of his magazines, stiff with his jizz. He had taken these panties, a delicacy he had begged for, and then paraded about in them like a prancing mummer, and had coarsely used and discarded them. He had treated her expensive gift as if they were little more than a catcher's mitt, and he had done so with absolutely no regard or respect for her. He hadn't even had the common decency to tidy up after himself.

But that, Judith reminded herself, is why she ruled over him. Robert needed it, badly, too. Somehow, his need to be directed and controlled was deeply embedded, acquired perhaps at his mother's feet and over her knees in his little boyhood, then long sublimated, only to blossom during adulthood as an erotic peculiarity—one that made for her pleasure.

Right about now, Judith thought, *he'll think I haven't been rough enough with him.*

She knew Robert well. She knew he would silently stew as he scrubbed their entire set of pots and pans, whether they were dirty or not, unhappy that she hadn't, on finding the mess and seeing him come from the shower, toweling his hair, picked up the nearest hairbrush and taken it to his ass. Oh, but he was so easy, so predictable, and he always wanted it so easily and so predictably. But that wasn't how she operated.

That he had yet to accept that fact made him all the more deserving of the pots and pans—and what was yet to come.

Judith heard the dishwasher rumble, old thing that it was, and smiled, satisfied that Robert had loaded it as required before

starting on the pots and pans. As one more crack of an aluminum bat and the attendant cheer of the crowd reached her, Judith told herself that Robert might grumble now, but he'd later
cheer just like that distant crowd.

She returned to her reading, a domestic novel that detailed
the interwoven struggles of various characters, starting in post-
war Britain and working in a backward timetable toward the
fiery, fearful Blitz, and though its sense of domesticity was far
more distant in time and far tamer in tenor than her own, she
enjoyed it with the same lush curiosity that she had for Robert.

Yes, he remained a curiosity to her. Judith had not grown to
adulthood with the kind of erotic neuroses that Robert carried,
but she had grown up amid feminism, with women in power,
and this pairing of male meekness and feminine authority was,
she thought, fine, even if it merged unexpected complements.
For all her bravado, Judith actually enjoyed Robert's tendencies
and never tired of matching them with a flexing of her own authority. It made the sexual side of their marriage a blissful and
heady endeavor.

Within seconds of kitchen silence, Robert appeared at the
door to the deck.

"I've finished with the kitchen, Ma'am," he reported, careful
to draw Judith from her book with sincerity and with none of
the melodrama he was often prone to.

Judith looked up from her book. A very naked-but-for-a-
woman's-apron Robert stood behind the door's screen, meekly
looking downward, his posture contrite. If not for the erection
that tented his apron, he would have been the perfect picture
of apology. Unfortunately, the stiff starch of the apron exagger-
ated his stiffy to the point of lampoonish caricature, and Judith
couldn't help but laugh. Robert blushed so red she could see it
even from behind the shadowed screen door.

Her laugh was brief and faded into renewed sternness. Judith motioned to the glass on the table beside her lounge chair and beckoned Robert to her side with a "My drink needs refreshing." Then she stopped him in his tracks with her next requirement.

"There's a pile of clothes in a laundry basket in our bedroom. It needs ironing. Bring the clothes, the iron, and the ironing board out here."

A look of panic overtook Robert, and Judith knew the thoughts behind his reaction.

"Yes," she confirmed. "Out here. On the deck, where all the neighbors might see."

"But—"

"But nothing," she snapped. She usurped his worry and would brook no argument.

Judith pretended her novel was more absorbing than Robert, yet she clandestinely glanced up from the pages of her book to catch him nervously scanning the perimeter of their backyard, wary of neighbors. Still in his apron and still sporting his ludicrous erection, Robert pressed iron to fabric, at once terrified of discovery yet thrilled to be such a pantywaist. Judith fought back the urge to smile, unwilling to reveal how enticing Robert appeared to her in this dilemma of her direction and his own making. Maintaining the appearance of stern distance would, after all, enhance Robert's discomfort, and it was his distress that kept this scene of theirs moving.

That, and the fact that Judith would, for the third week in a row, avoid having to iron a damn thing.

Robert's needs certainly kept life lively, and although they could at times provoke Judith into a disciplinary mode, she had long ago abandoned the question of who was really on top. Yes, his needs could prompt her to action, but Robert did little more than sway the drift of any given day, because once Judith reacted, Judith took charge. Robert might act out, but it was Judith who orchestrated every move thereafter. It was Judith who put Robert through these embarrassing paces and potentially compromising positions. It was Judith who delighted as Robert endured.

Generations ago, before women took up the mantle of feminism and broke away from the façade of domestic bliss, women like Judith had a name: battle axe. The label was leveled with scorn, and "battle axes" were depicted as big, brutish beasts who towered over their cowering, puny, sycophantic husbands. But behind the distain for such things was a hidden reality: Some men needed women warriors to lord it over them. And some women enjoyed doing so.

Judith certainly did. She not only enjoyed putting Robert into delightfully humiliating and trying circumstances, but she reveled in the erotic anticipation that built as her episodic scenes unfolded. The look of unease on Robert's face as he struggled in his emasculated state, the hiss of the iron, the peek of nipple that shyly revealed itself from behind the apron as Robert worked, all of it readied Judith for more. All of it made her lust for more.

But one could not rush these things. One had to keep to the discipline to get to the reward.

And so Judith kept to her plan and kept her nose in her book. But she was no longer able to read a single sentence without distraction. She drifted into idle thought, all of which centered on what next she would require of Robert. And this made her like the steam hissing from Robert's iron: wet and hot.

Judith assessed Robert's finished efforts from her lounge chair, rifling through the basket of pressed and folded clothing just enough to appear thorough. Robert hung on her scrutiny like a child before a mother's inspection of a newly made bed or a student beneath a teacher's peering examination of a penmanship exercise. His expression was both pained and anticipatory. He was at once dreading her opinion and praying for her approval, and his cock, now half limp, reflected his conflicted state.

Once, then twice, Judith lifted a corner of the clothing pile and let it riffle back into place. Finally, she opined.

"Your technique is much improved. Your ironing is thorough, the folding careful and attentive. And you've become quite accomplished at neatly stacking everything. Quite adept, compared to where you began."

Robert shuffled from foot to foot bashfully, and a smile surfaced on his downward gaze—Judith could only glimpse the curled ends of it—indicating his happy receipt of such news.

"Thank you, Ma'am."

"You're welcome. Now pick up after yourself and put all this away."

As Robert turned and stepped away, taking the basket with him, Judith added, "Bring the spoon with you on your way back."

Robert's steps faltered only slightly when her words hit him. He groaned and hoisted the basket discretely higher, subtle responses that told Judith that his erection had returned. Eagerly, she acted to squash it.

"Yes, you're doing far better with the laundry," she mused. "If only you were as attentive and responsible with my undergarments. If only you kept your porn picked up and respected my belongings as well."

The groan that escaped Robert this time was more agony than ecstasy.

He returned bearing the spoon. Its handle was long and its bowl broad and sturdy, just the thing needed for seeking contrition. Robert knew its sting well and, although it was not always a pleasant thing, it was often necessary. What Judith deemed, Judith received. Dutifully, he surrendered the implement to her.

Judith took the spoon in hand, then ordered Robert to make her seat as upright as possible.

"One can lounge over a good read, but one must work over a bad boy," she claimed, setting her novel aside.

Robert glanced about, aware that he was about to turn his ass toward the backyards of at least two neighbors. Catching him yet again, Judith finally commented about his skittishness.

"I wouldn't worry about your ass and the neighbors, if I were you. I'd worry about your ass over my knee. You've much to pay for."

Robert's eyes went wide, he blushed profusely, and although he opened his mouth, apparently his throat had gone too dry to allow any response in the form of words.

"Cat got your tongue?" Judith demanded.

It was, of course, a rhetorical question and when Judith patted her thigh, Robert merely nodded, knelt down, and placed himself across her lap. As his apron fell forward and exposed his backside, Judith caressed Robert's ass. It was small and firm—unfairly so, she thought, that men should, on the whole, have smaller, firmer rumps than women—but the twitch of his muscles put a sly smile across her face. Robert shifted his weight once, then again. Apparently, assuming the position across her lap via a lounge chair was not the most comfortable way to receive punishment.

Judith pressed the flat of her hand into Robert's back and pushed down.

"Stop squirming. This is your correction and you're to take

your lumps however they come—even if it's lumpy beneath you."

A throb swiped the side of Judith's thigh—Robert's cock, responding to her chastising words—and she laughed, loud and with so little restraint that she came close to cackling. *Wait until I'm an old crone,* she thought, gazing at a trembling Robert. *Wait until I have you in my clutches then.*

Without announcement or instruction, Judith raised the spoon and brought it down hard on Robert's ass. It sounded sharply, a smack so unmistakable that anyone would recognize it as comeuppance. Robert grunted at the impact. The pain was not enough to move him and, knowing this, Judith applied three swift, fierce whacks to him—all in the same spot over his left cheek. On the last strike, Robert lurched and cried out.

"You'll tidy up after yourself from now on, won't you?" she demanded.

"Yes, Ma'am," Robert answered, his voice breathy.

Four more whacks, this time to the right cheek. Again Robert reacted, and both of his ass cheeks now blazed with the red imprint of the spoon.

"And you'll never use my possessions again in your diddling, will you?"

Robert whimpered and hesitated—as Judith knew he would. He had never been able to squash his panty fetish for long. Judith acted on his indecision and paddled both ass cheeks relentlessly, letting up only when Robert choked on the pain and growled like a trapped animal.

"You'll never use my possessions again in your diddling, will you?" she repeated. "Answer quickly, or else—"

The "or else" was the spoon, resting between his legs. Against his balls.

"I promise!" Robert sputtered. "I won't!"

Delightful, Judith thought. *Absolutely delightful.* She patted his sack with the spoon, pleased, and enjoyed the small grunts that punctuated the strokes—Robert reacting. But Robert's discipline didn't end simply because the admission she sought finally came her way. No, Judith would have to drive home the point. This time, the paddling lasted beyond the bright spots each cheek sported, beyond Robert's lurching and reacting, beyond Judith's arm tiring. It lasted until all of Robert's ass blazed red, until it was hot to her touch. Judith knew that Robert would consider this storm of strokes the final phase of correction.

But it wasn't.

Setting aside the spoon and without any praise for Robert's endurance, Judith issued one final, humiliating instruction.

"Tomorrow, on your way home from work, you will stop at the dollar store. You know, the one near the pet store. On the far wall, look for their clothing essentials—socks, handkerchiefs, and the like. There's a column of women's panties there, gaudy things. They look like what your grandmother would wear...if she worked as a stripper. Buy one of each."

She paused, imagining Robert before the cashiers—two men who always seemed to be there, working all hours of the day—blushing and fumbling over his purchase. Then she imagined him blushing and fumbling before her.

"When you return home, lay them out on the bed, remove whichever one you consider the most humiliating from its packaging. Set it on the bed, strip naked, kneel, and wait for me. We'll see what comes next when I find you waiting."

What comes next. Judith knew, too, what—or rather, who—would come next: she now, he tomorrow. She pushed Robert from her lap and put him on his knees. She lifted the skirt of her dress high and beckoned him with a glimpse of her cunt. Eagerly, he dove to it, his mouth to its plenty, and set to pleasure her. Judith let her dress fall back into place and hide Robert beneath its fabric.

Returning to her novel, Judith said nothing more to Robert, but as she read, she heard their neighbors. Their voices came from behind the privacy shield they had erected alongside the hot tub on their deck, and she wondered how long they had been outside. *Had they heard the smack of the spoon?* she wondered. After a particularly loud shout came from across the backyard, Robert moaned, aware of them too.

Still, Judith said nothing.

She would say nothing until Robert's tongue left her no choice and she clenched her thighs against his face and came loudly enough that it would hush her neighbors and leave Robert flustered with embarrassment. She did not know if he blushed—she did not let him up from between her legs—and if her neighbors stole a peek from over their privacy shield, they'd spy him sprawled there, naked and half-hidden. They'd see Judith immersed in a good book, poised as if there was nothing unusual in this backyard scenario.

Smiling, Judith read on, in full control and loving every minute of it.

THE MISTRESS MEETS HER MATCH

Kristina Wright

They come to me like starving men, willing to do whatever I bid them to do. With the arch of an eyebrow or the flick of a knot-tipped leather whip, they're mine to command. When they leave me, they are grateful, exhausted, and a little bit poorer. I am a professional dominatrix and I make no apologies.

I came to this profession the same way an undertaker or a farmer comes to theirs: I was born to it. No, my mother wasn't a dominatrix. She was headmistress at an exclusive boarding school for girls, nestled in a small town in the hills of Vermont. I learned the look—the one that can make a man tremble or come in his pants—from my mother. I learned the walk—back rigid, eyes straight ahead—from her, as well. At my mother's knee I learned that discipline demands a price, and that price is pain.

My clients know me only as Mistress Katarina, a woman with a curvaceous body, jet-black hair, and sparkling green eyes that never, ever cry. They are the ones who cry. They cry for mercy, they cry to come, they cry for more. Always more.

Among those who visit me are two attorneys, one gynecologist, three police officers, and a city councilman. They come cloaked in guilt—or is it shame?—reluctant at first to reveal themselves. That changes within the hour. By the time they have my stiletto heel rubbing up the length of their cocks, they are willing to sell me their souls. I don't take souls in trade, but I do accept MasterCard, Visa, and American Express. Cash is nice, too.

If you've never squeezed a man's balls in your hand and seen the terror in his eyes, you haven't known power. If you've never cracked a whip and watched a man flinch, you haven't known anticipation. And if you've never had a man grovel at your feet, you haven't known what it means to be a bitch goddess. These men who come to me, hearts pounding, cocks hard, know who I am and they know what they want. Because I am a benevolent bitch goddess, I usually give them what they want, but not before they suffer.

I came the first time a man begged for mercy while I whipped him. It was the most amazing sensation and I was nearly faint with the effort to remain standing and continue the session. I have always suspected I was more easily aroused than the average woman, but to come without being touched, to come without even thinking about coming—now, that was a heady experience. I barely acknowledged my grateful slave as I crumpled into a chair and slid my hand beneath the leather crotch of my panties. There, glistening on my fingertips, was proof of my arousal.

I'd fallen into being a dominatrix because of a need to pay my bills, and yet I'd found something much more rewarding—personal fulfillment. From then on, I reveled in the feel of the whip or crop in my hand, the cries of men who desired pleasure in the form of pain. It became as addictive as a drug, this ability to control men. I discovered that not only was I good at it, I needed it. It was enough, for a while.

I have been at this game for four years. I began to lose interest in the dynamics of power and control about three years into it. Around the same time, I began to lose interest in sex, which was more disturbing. I decided it was time to take my earnings and run, maybe open a bookstore that specialized in erotica and find my lost libido.

Then I met Stephen.

I was at a bookstore around the corner from the studio I work out of downtown—it's never a good idea to bring clients to the house, I've discovered—when I literally bumped into Stephen in the business and finance section. I'd just left the studio and a client I'd nicknamed Quick Draw McGraw because his sessions never took more than thirty minutes and he always paid for an hour. I was intent on finding a book about starting my own business when I turned a corner and ran right into a muscular chest that barely yielded, despite my full-frontal assault.

The guy gave me a long, appraising look even though I was only wearing jeans and an old college T-shirt. I never leave the studio in my dominatrix gear because it would be unseemly in this part of town, with its high-end lofts, hip restaurants, and pseudo-urban couples pushing baby strollers and drinking pricey coffee, for me to be seen walking around in pleather miniskirts and thigh-high boots. I'd chosen the area for precisely that reason: It would make the men who came to me more comfortable to be in a "better" neighborhood where they could be seen being conspicuous, plus it would afford me a certain amount of safety. Rent was reasonable because I rented space over a deli that closed at five, which meant privacy wasn't usually an issue because most of my appointments were in the evening. I had a private entry to accommodate weekend clients and the "early bird" specials who wanted an afternoon quickie. To anyone who asked, I was an artist using the space as a private studio. Almost no one ever asked.

Stephen and I made our apologies and I started to pass him, but his voice stopped me in my tracks.

"Business slow today?"

I immediately went into Mistress Katarina mode. My spine straightened and my hair swung as I whipped around. I looked at him again, convinced he was a former client I just hadn't recognized. It wasn't likely; I have an excellent memory for faces and men who have served me, but it was possible. He didn't look familiar, though.

"Excuse me? Do I know you?"

He smiled easily. "No. I know one of your, um, clients."

"Oh, you mean one of my art patrons?"

His eyes narrowed. "No, *mistress,* one of your 'dates.' He said you were worth every penny."

Crap. I hated having to deal with business in my free time. "If you'd like to schedule an appointment, I can give you my card," I said, just as coldly as I could manage after having been caught off guard.

"Actually, I'm not the submissive type. But I'll let you buy me coffee."

It's rare that a man leaves me speechless, but he did. I stood there in the business and finance section, open-mouthed and blinking. Realizing that he was serious, I started to laugh. He seemed nonplussed, waiting patiently until I caught my breath and could speak.

"Well, thanks, but no thanks."

He shrugged. "That's fine. I just figured you probably don't get an opportunity to meet many men who are your intellectual and emotional equals, and I thought we might hit it off."

His arrogance was irritating. It was also attractive. "I see. So, coffee with you would take care of the question of whether we'd hit it off?"

"No, I know we'd hit it off. Coffee would just facilitate the process to step two."

"Step two?"

He nodded. "Step two. And three. And four."

I was intrigued in spite of myself. "How many steps do you foresee in this little venture?"

He reached out and ran his fingers through my hair. "As many as it takes for you to let your guard down."

"Why would I do that?" The whole situation was starting to be more annoying than interesting. "Because you're perfect for me?"

"No. Because you're strung so tight I think you're going to snap something. You need to relax."

I don't know what made me say yes, but an hour later we were sitting in a coffee shop on the corner, swapping stories about our jobs. Stephen was a psychologist, and one of his patients had come to me in the past. He wouldn't say which one, only that he hadn't thought it was a bad idea and that he felt that my job served a valuable purpose. I was shocked, and pleased, by his approval.

Surprisingly, I didn't go to bed with Stephen until we'd gone out a few more times. I say *surprisingly* because I wanted to. Badly. It had been months since I'd even dated, and my lack of interest in sex hadn't really sent me looking for anyone. Yet Stephen managed to get me soaking wet every time he kissed me, so I was curious to find out what he could do to me in bed.

By the time I found out, I was so hot for him that I couldn't stand it. He stripped me slowly, taking his time with my body the way I liked. He touched and licked me and I eagerly returned the favor, anxious to feel his sizable cock inside me at last. When he finally slid into me, I was a quivering mass of nerve endings. Then something unbelievable happened: I lost interest. He was there, inside me, hard and throbbing and oh-so-filling and I had my arms and legs wrapped around him, my pussy so sloshing wet I thought he'd slip out despite his girth, and all I could do was stare at the ceiling fan over his shoulder and hope he finished soon.

Stephen noticed almost immediately. He stilled, pulling back to look at me. "What's wrong?"

I feigned a smile. "Nothing. You feel incredible," I murmured.

"Kate," he said, and it was a warning. "Something's wrong. What did I do?"

"Nothing," I said, honestly, trying to hold him to me even while he was pulling free. "Really. It's just been a while, and my mind is distracted."

He rolled over beside me. "Yeah, well, you shouldn't be distracted while I'm fucking you."

I knew he was right, but it didn't keep me from being irritated. "So why don't you go home and I can be distracted by myself?"

"Yes, *mistress*." He got out of bed and got dressed before I had time to contemplate what his snide comment had made me feel. "I'll call you."

I didn't expect to hear from him, but I did. So I apologized for snapping at him, and he apologized for pushing the issue. He suggested we'd rushed into bed too soon, though it had been six weeks since we first met and a little voice in my head whispered that that wasn't it at all. We went out a couple of more times and didn't do anything more than make out in the front seat of his car before he dropped me off. I wanted him, really *wanted* him, dammit, and I was determined to have him.

The next time we went to bed, it was at my house. I was

convinced that the combination of being in a new place with a new guy had been the problem. I was wrong. This time when we went to bed, despite Stephen's spending a long, long time licking and teasing my body, nothing happened. I didn't even get wet. Nothing. It was the single most embarrassing, frustrating, horrifying moment of my life. I suddenly knew what it felt like to be a guy who loses his erection.

"I am so sorry," I apologized, again and again. "I don't know what's wrong with me."

"Maybe you're thinking about work," he said. He didn't sound angry, just confused.

"I learned a long time ago to leave work at the studio." I sighed. "My sex drive just hasn't been what it used to be. Maybe being a dominatrix killed my sex drive."

He propped himself up on one elbow and stared at me. "Or maybe you can take Kate out of the studio, but you can't take Mistress Katarina out of Kate."

"What are you talking about?"

"Being a dominatrix isn't just your job, Kate," he said. "It's who you are. You need to be in charge."

I shook my head. "That's not true. I've never dominated a man in bed before."

"And how great has your sex life been up to this point?"

I considered his question. He was right. My sex life had never been anything spectacular. I'd had a good time, sure, but nothing that even came close to approaching the rush I got dominating a man in my studio. The thought was unsettling. Was he right? Did I need to be in charge? I hadn't thought so, but maybe he was on to something. In which case, our relationship—not to mention our sex life—was doomed.

"It won't work," I said. "You told me yourself you're not the submissive type."

"Then I guess you'd better figure out how to make me the submissive type."

It seemed we were at an impasse. His cock had gone flaccid while we were arguing and I was suddenly irritated. How dare he make me think about work, when all I wanted to do was get laid?

I stood up and paced naked across my bedroom floor. I felt like I was being put on the spot. All I wanted was good sex with a guy I was really attracted to. Was I going to have to work for it? Then I remembered the little tingle I'd gotten when Stephen had called me "mistress" the last time we'd tried this. I'd been angry with him, but still felt a sense of satisfaction. Arousal.

I was conscious of his watching me from the bed. He looked concerned, thoughtful, but his limp penis taunted me. I went into the bathroom and slammed the door. I stared at myself in the mirror. I looked like a startled doe, and that's the way I felt. Maybe Stephen had discovered something about myself that I hadn't known—or hadn't wanted to admit: that being in control wasn't just a way to make a living, it's what I actually needed in my sex life.

I slipped on my red satin robe that hung on the bathroom door and went back into the bedroom. Stephen was where I'd left him on the bed. He watched me carefully, no doubt wondering if I was going to burst into tears or demand that he leave.

"Come here, Stephen," I said softly.

He hesitated a moment, as if sensing that some sort of change had occurred. Then he stood up and walked to me. "Are you okay?"

Instead of answering his question, I asked one of my own. "Do you want me?"

We were standing close, but not touching. He reached out and stroked my hair. "You know I do. Do you want me?"

"Yes. On my terms."

His hand dropped from my hair. "What does that mean?"

"Get on your knees, Stephen."

Again, he hesitated. It had been his idea for me to take charge, but I knew he was struggling with relinquishing control. I felt a little thrill at the challenge of breaking him.

"I know this is what you need, Kate, but I have to warn you—"

I cut him off. "Get on your knees, Stephen."

He knelt. I smiled. I was going to enjoy this. With any luck, he would too.

"Good." I stroked his cheek with my fingertips, feeling the rush of anticipation I felt whenever a man knelt before me. Of course, Stephen was the first one I'd ever wanted to fuck. "Open my robe."

He looked up at me, then at my waist. Slowly, he untied the sash and parted my robe. "You're beautiful."

"Do you want to fuck me?"

He took a deep breath. "Yes."

I slapped him. Not hard, but hard enough so that he would know I was serious. "You don't have to call me 'mistress' and my name to you is Kate, not Katarina, but you will show respect."

He stared into my eyes. "Yes, *ma'am.*"

"Good." I realized his cock had hardened. I sat down on the edge of the bed and spread my legs. "Stand up."

He stood, cock swollen and heavy against his thigh.

"Come closer." Once he was close enough for me to touch, I said, "Stroke yourself."

"What?"

I slapped his cock the way I'd slapped his face. Not hard enough to hurt him, or make him lose his erection, but enough that he wouldn't make that mistake again.

"Sorry," he muttered. "Yes, ma'am."

He was annoyed, embarrassed, and fighting his own sexual desire because of it. I had to make him stop thinking about what was happening and just *feel*. I could already sense my own body responding to the shift in dynamics. I could feel the wetness growing between my thighs, the heavy, engorged feeling building in my cunt. It was the same feeling I got dominating men in my studio, only there was never any physical contact and, with the exception of that first time, no physical release for me. Knowing that this time, finally, I would get fucked, get to come, get to feel everything, made my pulse quicken. I wanted Stephen, but I wanted him to want me just as much.

I had a thought. "Did you masturbate that night after we tried to have sex?"

He nodded.

"Stroke yourself like you did that night," I commanded. "Show me what you did to release all the tension you couldn't release with me."

He opened his mouth as if to argue, but promptly closed it. I didn't know if it was because he didn't want to get slapped again or because he was getting too aroused to fight me anymore. In any case, he wrapped his hand around his cock and began stroking it.

There's something about watching a man jerk off that turns me on. Maybe it's because it's so different than the way I masturbate. Men have more flesh to work with, more to touch and look at. I can touch myself, but I can't really watch unless there are mirrors involved.

"That's it," I said. "Stroke your cock."

Stephen stared into my eyes while he masturbated, occasionally glancing down at his own cock as if he couldn't believe he was doing this in front of me.

I let him jerk off for a few minutes, knowing he was probably too self-conscious to orgasm, which wasn't my goal. I wanted him to stay hard long enough for his brain to shut off, as I knew it would.

Finally, I was rewarded with a liquid pearl of pre-come on the tip of his cock. "Stop," I commanded.

He stroked himself two more times before he stopped. "Sorry, ma'am."

I let his disobedience slide. "How do you feel?"

He didn't hesitate. "I want to fuck you so bad it hurts."

"I don't care what you want," I said. "Maybe I'll just let you masturbate until you come all over the floor."

"Whatever you want, ma'am."

I laughed. "Tell me what you'll do to me if I let you fuck me."

"Anything you want me to do," he said, and I knew he meant it. He hesitated. "Please let me fuck you—Kate."

I wanted to press for more explicit details, but I was going easy on him. This time. I leaned forward and touched the tip of my tongue to the tip of his cock. I pulled back, slowly, taking his pre-come with me in a string that connected my tongue to his cock. He groaned. I looked up at him, saw the sheer lust in his expression, and realized he was mine.

I licked my lips, tasting him. "Put the tip of your cock inside me."

He knelt on the edge of the bed between my thighs and guided his cock toward my cunt. Slowly, so slowly that I wanted to scream, he pushed the head of his cock between my lips.

"Just a little deeper," I breathed. "Go slow, Stephen."

He pushed another inch into me, and I could hear him gritting his teeth as if he could barely keep from thrusting the entire length inside me.

I clenched my muscles around him. He felt so good, but I had no intention of letting him have what he wanted until I wanted it, too. "Pull out."

He was so focused on watching what he was doing to me that he didn't seem to hear me at first. "Ma'am?"

"Now, Stephen," I demanded. "Take your cock out of me and stand up."

He obeyed without protest. Sweat glistened on his forehead and his breathing was a little ragged.

I sat up, trying to control my own erratic breathing. His cock was shiny with my arousal. I leaned forward and licked the head of it, tasting myself. "I want you to listen to me, Stephen," I said, giving his cock another lick. "When I tell you to stop, you will stop. Understand?"

"Yes, ma'am," he all but groaned as I took the head of his cock between my lips. "I'm sorry. It won't happen again."

I released him from my mouth. "When I tell you to fuck me, I want you to fuck me, Stephen." I ran a fingertip over the head of his cock and up the shaft and back down again. His cock twitched. "I want you to fuck me hard and deep. I want you to fuck me in every position I demand, in every orifice I offer, as many times as I like until I tell you to stop. Can you do that, Stephen?"

He looked into my eyes, his expression one of barely contained lust. "Yes, ma'am. I'll fuck you. Just say the word and I will fuck you any way you want."

I stared at him for a long, long moment, my fingertip resting on the tip of his cock. "Fuck me, Stephen," I said softly. "Fuck me now."

He was inside me before I got out the last word. He fucked me hard and deep, his cock slamming into me over and over until I was gasping and screaming and coming. I clung to him as he used my body the way I wanted, the way I'd demanded, the way I'd been missing for so long.

Someday soon, I will retire as Mistress Katarina and became simply Kate, the bookstore owner. I'll still be in charge, just in a different way. Stephen will take care of my need to dominate in the bedroom and, when I'm feeling generous, I'll take care of his need to occasionally be the boss. I am a benevolent bitch goddess, after all.

WAITING FOR ME

MinaRose

"As if the shit-ass day I had wasn't bad enough," I said out loud to myself, gritting my teeth and grinding my clenched fists around the steering wheel. "Fuck you!" I screamed to no one in particular as the little green sports car wedged itself into the barely existing space between me and the car ahead. I laid on my horn, as if the driver could hear it over the obnoxious *thump-thump-thump* of his car stereo. I rubbed my temples with one hand and took a deep breath.

I hate days like this. The only thing holding my nerves together as I fought the god-awful traffic was the image of my husband, Gary, on his knees at the door waiting for me. *He better be there, he better be ready for what's coming to him. He better have a drink ready for me, or I'm going to take it out on his ass.*

I flicked my turn signal with just a tad more force than was necessary and prepared to force my way over across the traffic moving at a snail's pace. By the time I got all the way over, I had to cut a wide corner of grass to get into the off-ramp. *Fucking jerks can't even let a girl get off.* Oh, but I was going to get off all right. I just had to get home first.

Once I left the damn highway it only took me about five minutes to get home.

I always go in through the garage. The door's going up gives Gary a little extra time to prepare himself for me. Gary's a stay-at-home guy. He runs his business part time out of the house, making more than double what most full-time men bring home. He cooks, cleans, shops, and does all the other shit I hate, because he knows how much I love my career, and he knows how much trouble he'd be in if he didn't take care of me.

I stalled for time in the car, taking a few minutes to check my hair and makeup, trying to tone down my hostility a bit.

When I cracked the door open he was there. God, he's so hot! Gary's blond, with strong features and an even stronger body. It always tightens things low in my body to see him kneeling on the floor, just inside the laundry room door, wearing only jeans, a leather collar, and a glowing grin. Today was no exception. His pants were so tight they looked like they'd been painted onto his body, and it was obvious he was happy to see me.

Just as I had hoped, there was a little silver tray in his hands with a single red rose and a Bay Breeze.

"Welcome home, Mistress," he said. I ruffled his loose, short curls as I reached for my drink. He closed his eyes, relishing my touch. I took my drink from his tray, dropped my briefcase on the floor, and put my right boot up on a little stool by the door, there for just such purposes. Gary set the tray down and crawled to my feet. The bare expanse of his back stretched before me as he bowed low, the very top of his ass crack a tease at his waistband. Carefully, using just his teeth, he unbuckled the boot, then, once I had kicked it off, he carried it to the shoe rack a few feet away. He repeated the process with my other boot, then tended to my briefcase and the drink tray.

I strutted through the kitchen into the living room where I watched him serve me with satisfaction. "You are such a good boy," I told him as he returned to my side. "Now," I said, downing the rest of my drink and setting the glass on a side table, "get me out of these clothes."

I followed his ass, which sways so nicely when he's on all fours, into the bedroom. I stood in the center of the open floor with my hands on my hips. Gary crawled around to my backside and came to his feet just long enough to reach the zipper high on my back with his teeth, then returned to his knees, taking my dress with him. Underneath my clothes I wore a sexy satin and lace push-up bra with matching panties and garters to hold up my thigh-highs. Gary carried my dress by its zipper to the hamper without looking up at me, then promptly returned, giving me just enough time to slip into my spiked-heel shoes. The expression on his face was priceless as he returned and took in the sight of me standing there in my lace, lingerie, and heels. This was going to be fun.

He knelt before me, rolling his eyes upward in a truly beautiful gesture of utter subservience. The first hint of heat and moisture began between my thighs as I watched this powerful, successful business guru lower himself in my presence.

"Mistress, you are stunning," he said, voice barely above a whisper. "How may I serve you this evening?"

"Get up on the bed," I commanded. "On your back, and hang your head over the side." He wasted no time jumping up onto the bed like a sexy puppy and assuming the position I wanted. He watched me approach him, upside-down, with wide, anticipatory eyes. I could do just about anything to him and he would beg me for more. I schooled my expression as I approached the bed, not wanting to reveal how much I needed this tonight.

I spread my legs and stood directly over Gary's face. I watched his dick grow within the confines of his pants to a sizable bulge. Just the thought of serving me had made him so hard that the fabric of his jeans strained to accommodate him.

"You know what I want you to do," I said. Without hesitation he buried his face into the crotch of my panties, inhaling deeply as if my scent were a drug. Then he began to work me. His tongue pressed playfully against me through the thin material of my underwear, his hot breath making me wet. He rubbed his tongue and lips along my crotch, mouthing me with incredible enthusiasm. Within minutes my panties were soaked and I was already near climax. I moaned, closing my eyes and enjoying the heaviness in my groin. The stress of the day dropped away from my body, leaving me relaxed as I settled into the building pulse of my pleasure.

Then Gary forgot himself. Sometimes I think he does it on purpose, as if he can tell that I don't want things to be over so quickly. Whether he did it intentionally, or just got caught up in the moment, Gary reached up with both hands and grabbed my hips, trying to force me further onto his mouth. Quick as a whip, I bent at the waist and spanked the huge bulge in his pants, not hard enough to really hurt, but I knew it stung. "Did I say you could touch me?" I asked, scorn in my voice.

"No, Mistress," he answered quickly with a quiver in his throat, "but you are so irresistible, I got carried away. I am so sorry, Mistress."

I spanked his dick again, this time getting a small sound out of him. "You're not sorry yet." I walked to the other side of the bed and undid his pants roughly, then tore them from his body. "Over," I barked. As he flipped onto his stomach I grabbed my cat-o'-nine tails that hangs from the bedpost.

Swift as lightning, I brought it down on Gary's bare backside, sharp and hard. Each little tail left a tiny red mark on his ass, and the sight of them brought a smile to my lips. I whipped him for at least five minutes, including the backs of his thighs in the fun. He struggled under the lashes and gave whimpering little yelps occasionally, but he took his punishment well. The whole time I admonished him through my grinning teeth. "Presumptuous slave ... *slap* ... thinks he can lay his hands on his mistress uninvited ... *smack* ... he will learn his lesson ... *whack* ... impertinent boy." I grew more and more excited as I whipped him and spoke the taunting words. My panties were soaked as my juices dripped from my throbbing pussy. When his ass and thighs were laid out in nice red welts, I swapped the cat-o'-nine tails for a little sack hanging from the same post.

"Over," I commanded, knowing that the fresh welts on the rough jacquard bedding would be uncomfortable as hell. Gary grimaced as he rolled, but his enjoyment of his punishment was betrayed by his rock-hard cock jutting straight out from his body. "What do you have to say for yourself?" I asked, loosening the drawstring on my little sack of toys.

"I am infinitely sorry, Mistress. Nothing I can say will excuse my error. I can only hope to make up for it by serving you flawlessly for the rest of the evening."

"Good answer," I said, slipping my panties down my legs, leaving just the garters and thigh-highs against my skin. I stuffed the soaked lace into his mouth, then removed a pair of leather cuffs from my bag. I buckled his wrists tightly together and then attached them to the loop on the front of his collar. I took my sweet time. "Don't touch," I said as I leaned back over his body, my dripping pussy in his face. He moaned through his gag when he saw the toy I took from my bag next.

I slipped a leather sleeve made of soft black ultrasuede around

his cock. I'd had the little device specially made to tease and torment him by squeezing his penis firmly and evenly, keeping him
hard, but giving him no opportunity for release. It laced up so
it was easy to tighten to the desired amount of pressure, like a
corset. I batted at his erection one more time as I tied the strings
tight and stood straight again. He squirmed his ass against the
bed, attempting to relieve some of the ache in his raw backside
and in his cock as it was squeezed by the toy he couldn't thrust
into, no matter how hard he tried.

In all his rolling and wriggling, Gary had scooted along the
bed so that his head no longer hung over the side. I crawled onto
the bed and straddled his face, my spiked heels digging into his
sides. I put my ass close to his bound hands and watched the
temptation build in his eyes. "Shall we try this again?" I asked,
squeezing my heels into him and bringing his face to me with a
handful of his curls. I removed my panties from between his lips.

"Yes, Mistress," he replied in a whisper. With nothing between me and his mouth, his breath teased my aching groin and
made my body tighten even more. He licked slowly along my
lips, not taking any liberties. After a few minutes of slow, careful
strokes, I pressed myself onto his face, forcing his tongue deeper.
That was all the encouragement he needed to eat me as if I was
his last meal.

I came all over his greedy mouth in a hot rush, my body writhing above him, riding his face like a rodeo cowgirl. "Mmmm,"
I moaned, my eyes still closed, my fists still wrapped in his hair.
"That was nice, but I'm not sure you've earned your pleasure
yet tonight. I think a little more punishment will do nicely." I
rubbed my ass against his still-bound hands, teasing, satisfied
when not a finger twitched to touch me back. I moved off him
to one side, making sure my spiked heel grazed under his chin as
it passed with enough pressure to either turn his head or hurt.

He chose to keep his head still, taking a sharp breath in through his teeth.

I surveyed him, his bound cock still waving in the air as he almost imperceptibly thrust his hips up off the bed in time with his growing need. He looked so helpless with his hands tethered to his collar, but not helpless enough. I released the cuffs from the collar and popped them apart. I fished between the mattress and headboard with my bare cheeks mere inches from Gary's face. He behaved himself until I found what I was looking for. The straps were always fastened around the bedposts; they just got stuffed down out of the way when we weren't using them. I brought them up and ordered Gary to the head of the bed. I used some fluffy down pillows to prop him into a half-sitting, half-lying-down position and hooked the straps separately to his cuffs, spreading his arms apart above his head.

Then I spread his legs wide with my hands and knelt between them with my knees spread, my heels tucked away for the moment under my butt. I began to touch myself, starting with my breasts. Gary loved this particular form of torture. It pained him not to be able to touch me or be touched, but his eager eyes gave away his enthusiasm for what was to come.

I grabbed both my breasts in my hands, squeezing them, working them in slow circles. I closed my eyes and arched my back just a little. I teased my nipples into rock-hard little points that poked against the silk of my bra. Moaning softly, I moved so that I straddled one of his legs. I began to thrust my hips and rub my aching groin on his thigh, pleasuring myself with him as if he were no more than a toy, a mere humping post.

I took care not to touch his cock as it jutted from him, still wrapped in leather, so close to my body. It swayed slightly with my movements, almost as if it were alive. I put two of my fingers into my mouth and sucked on them, seductively, then dropped that hand to rub my throbbing clit. Moisture ran down Gary's thigh as I played with myself. His face was so strained that it betrayed how much he wanted to be allowed to touch me. Now he was making small whimpering noises in his throat, pulling against his restraints as I used him for my own pleasure.

"Have you had enough, my little sex toy?" I asked with a long slow rub against his leg. He had to try twice before he could answer me.

"I am yours to do with as you please, Mistress. It is not my place to decide if my punishment has been enough."

"Good answer, slave. You are lucky that it is now my wish to pleasure you."

"Oh, *yes,* Mistress," Gary sighed softly as I moved a hand toward his cock. I gave it a playful slap, watching it bob back and forth like a punch-me clown. As I wrapped my hand around him, a loud groan escaped his lips and I was forced to stuff my soaking wet panties back in his mouth. He whimpered quietly while I teased his needy dick, running one finger up and down its length. As I barely stroked him, his legs began to bend at the knee as he squirmed beneath my hand.

"Keep still," I barked, punctuating the command with a rough slap to each of his thighs.

"Yeff Miffstwuss," he uttered, doing his best to speak around the satin and lace ball in his mouth.

I went back to playing with him and he closed his eyes and gave some effort to remaining still. I wrapped my whole hand around his penis and began to jack him off slowly, rubbing the leather sleeve against his sensitive skin. I had barely gotten start-ed when his knees came up off the bed again. I grabbed his balls in my hand and squeezed. "Do I need to help you stay still?" I warned, tweaking the loose flesh of his sac with two fingers. He nodded his head solemnly, too ashamed to even attempt a response. He was always disappointed in himself when he couldn't keep still for me, though truthfully, knowing that I could drive him that crazy brought a smile to my lips.

I brought his legs together with a barrage of alternating slaps, and then sat on his thighs, just above his knees. I put my heels out beside his hips so that I perched on him like a grasshopper, my knees wide in the air. He had a great view of my pussy, still slick from humping him but also getting wet again on its own. Spreading my legs like that always makes me so horny, and the further I spread, the hornier I get.

I put both hands between my legs and slowly loosened the laces on the cock sleeve. I drew it off his penis so slowly that he whimpered, just barely, through his gag. I roughly yanked the sleeve the rest of the way off and tossed it to the side. "I'll give you a reason to whimper," I teased him, settling myself down a little higher on his legs, spreading myself just a bit wider. I dug the heels of my stilettos into his hips, which brought a satisfying whine to his throat.

I grabbed his cock in one hand and it throbbed for me, springing to an even more impressive width. I stroked him, bringing my hand in close to my body so that my thumb passed over and over my clit as I pleasured him. I sighed with the contact and tried to touch myself as much as possible, watching Gary's eyes watching me. I reached behind my back and unclasped my bra with my free hand, wriggled out of the little lacy prison, then threw it off the bed. I rubbed my breast, teasing it in slow circles while my other hand masturbated us both. I pinched and twisted my nipple until it stood plump and erect again, then switched to the other breast.

I wanted both my hands free. I lifted myself up slightly and positioned my legs with my knees down in the mattress, heels harmless near Gary's knees. I set myself down on top of him so that he was trapped between us. His dick pulsed against me, bringing my breath to a gasp. I began to work my hips so that I slid over and over him, my slick nether lips hugging his cock. Back and forth I rode him, both hands running over my breasts, softly at first, teasing, then more intensely as the orgasm began to build in me.

Gary's eyes got heavy lidded as he watched me, panting through his gag. He thrust his hips as much as he could under my weight. I took him into me without warning, forcing myself down onto his impressive width. Both our breaths came out in a rush as he filled me. For a moment I didn't move, I just let myself widen to accept him, took him as deeply into me as he would go. He groaned beneath me from the sensation of being inside me after so much foreplay.

I started to rock my hips against Gary's body slowly, so slowly, savoring the full feeling in my groin as his long cock brushed against the end of me. Our breaths quickened in unison as my rhythm sped up. My movements above him were like a dance, a back-and-forth, an in-and-out movement that became an all-out pounding as I came closer to my release. Gary's moans became so frantic that I removed the gag from his mouth so he could draw breath fast enough.

"Mistress," he gasped," I am so close … please … may I come?" his words squeezed out between pants.

"Not yet," I told him, thrusting deeper and slower now. "Not yet … close … close … close." I was murmuring in time with my movements.

"Mistress, I can't hold back anymore. Please, please, please," he begged me quietly.

His pleading pushed me over the edge and I screamed, "Now! *Oh God!*" as I came. Gary's orgasm exploded hot inside me as he shouted wordlessly, pounding his hips upward into me as fast and hard as he could. Wave after wave of pleasure took us as noises that were hardly human spilled from our mouths.

As the orgasm neared its end, I twisted my hips and flexed my muscles in a maneuver that brought a fresh climax to both of us. The second one lasted even longer than the first as I tightened around Gary and rode his body mercilessly. When the last drop of pleasure was spent, I collapsed at Gary's side and struggled to catch my breath.

When I could see straight again, I looked over at Gary to find him grinning at me, wearing nothing but his leather collar and restraints, panting like a golden retriever with his tongue hanging from his mouth. It was so goofy I started to laugh and couldn't stop. He laughed with me until we were both short of breath again. I moved to the head of the bed to release him from his bonds, then gathered him up in my arms. I kissed the top of his sweaty head and gave his bare ass a swat as he put his arms around my waist. He looked up at me, that submissive look of belonging and contentment, and I kissed him. I kissed and licked at his mouth in a gesture so much softer than anything we had done all evening. When I finally released him, he settled his head into the curve of my neck and kissed me lightly there.

"How was your day?" Gary asked me softly.

"I don't remember," I replied, kissing the top of his golden head again.

THE INNER VIXEN

Saskia Walker

Daniel is kneeling before me. I walk around him, my paces measured, my long leather boots making a quiet but insistent sound as they brush together. They're all I'm wearing. Daniel is stripped to the waist, his arms cuffed behind him. I'm admiring his body, so leanly muscular as he kneels on the floor before me, resting on his haunches, his torso upright and proud. As I consider the fact that he is mine, my willing pet, power plumes through me. As if it were a heady sexual elixir, I thrive on it. My core tightens and my sex grows damper with each passing moment.

His head moves imperceptibly as he watches me, and I revel in his adoring gaze. His cock is hard inside his faded black jeans, but I know he likes that confinement, just as he likes his wrists bound behind his back while I survey him. He's so alert, so taut with restrained desire. I feel it pouring out of him and it empowers me more.

As I walk on, circling him, I reach over, pull a chair close behind him, and sit. Over his shoulder, I see our reflection in the mirror. He's looking too, and it's the perfect image of woman and lover.

I trace one hand down his back. His muscles ripple and I know he's longing for more, for a more vivid assault on his senses: the whip. Making him wait, I sit back in the chair, lift my foot, and rest one stiletto heel between his shoulder blades, edging him forward. He pivots against it and groans aloud, his body arched. I know just how much pain he wants, how much he needs. My body responds to his reaction, heat rising to the surface of my skin. My inner vixen is revving up to full throttle, the essential me—the inner woman that Daniel recognized and introduced me to.

"How did you know that I would respond?" I asked him the night we met.

"I saw her, your inner vixen. I wanted to know her. I wanted to experience her."

So did I.

That's how it began.

We met at an alternative music event. I was there to photograph it for a guide promoting local gigs. I went alone, which I usually did when I was working. I dressed strong, which meant people wouldn't bother me—Doc Martens, black combat pants with a studded belt, cropped sports bra, bare midriff, my tribal tattoos on display.

It was a hot night and heat was rising from the pavement. Inside the pub venue I found the performance room was a large space upstairs, filling fast with the alternative crowd, black-wearing fetishists and goths. I stationed myself by a pillar near the front, where I had a good view of both stage and audience. The atmosphere was already humming with energy when the music kicked off.

I was busy photographing the first band when I became aware of someone watching me. I scanned the crowd. The man caught my eye and, as he did, he acknowledged me, quickly smiling and walking over. All in black, he was a studious type with shaggy hair and a lean, whip-strong countenance.

He ducked in against my head to speak over the music, introducing himself, commenting on what I was up to. "Nice camera, is this a hobby?"

"Started that way. It's work, this time around. I'm photographing the gig for a new music magazine."

He nodded. "I haven't seen you in the scene before."

"I just moved from the other side of London." I nodded my head to the people behind him. "Looks like a fun crowd."

"You better believe it." His smile held so much mischief that I was immediately affected by it.

Looking back at how events unfolded that night, I often contemplate how surprised I would have been if I had known where it was going. I tried not to get too distracted from the job as I answered his questions. There was something compelling about him but I couldn't put my finger on it. Was it because he was looking so attentively at me?

During the gap between the bands I took a break to chat properly. He started to talk about astronomy, of all things. He was intelligent and amusing, and I was quickly laughing, unable to stop enjoying the rapid-fire conversation he initiated. The crowd moved around us, a parade of peacocks, a blur of black, velvet, shiny, metal-studded—a visual feast for the senses. The DJ music between the bands had my pulse racing, or was it because of Daniel's attention and the fact it was all mine? All mine. Like a devotee. Oh, yes, I was hooked, even though I didn't yet know why.

When he made the move, he did it subtly, never breaking his

conversation. He reached inside his biker jacket and pulled out a small, soft leather object. He turned it in his hands, attracting my attention to it. I saw that it was a leather head mask. He looked up suddenly, and stopped talking.

He was measuring my reaction to the object he held.

My pulse tripped and then raced on, fascination flickering inside me.

His eyes narrowed, glinting, his smile wickedly mischievous and attractive. I couldn't stop myself from returning it. Behind him I saw that people were looking our way. Part of me wanted to walk away. Whatever game he was playing with me right there at the front of the venue was going to attract attention. But he triggered something inside me, and it was because of his demeanor, somehow respectful, and intrinsically sexy. It tugged at my curiosity, and aroused me.

"Will you lace me in?" He paused, his eyes scrutinizing me as I considered the remark.

Something was unfolding inside me, and it was something big, overwhelming.

I nodded, still smiling. I'd never done anything like this before, but the adventure had me firmly in its grasp. He pulled the mask over his head. It moved easily into place, pushing his hair down and outlining his head starkly. The leather was polished black, reflecting the stage lights as he turned and dipped down to let me tie the laces that ran down the back of his skull to the nape of the neck.

Oh, how that simple act affected me, fuelling me for what was to come.

My camera dangled from my neck as I moved into place. The laces felt good in my hands, and I enjoyed the feeling of control I got when I pulled the soft leather into place. It hugged tightly to his skull, enclosing him. Even though I tried to concentrate on the task, I was acutely aware of my own reaction to it, as well as the attention we were generating from the crowd beyond. People were watching, and somehow that made it all the more arousing.

When I was done, he turned back to me, his eyes twinkling through the peepholes. Incredibly, he unzipped the mouth and continued his conversation as before. The second band came on-stage. The singer, a striking punk in leather jeans and a studded corset, strutted the stage as she sang, twin keyboard players behind her moving to the drum and bass sound. Daniel and I shifted to the music at first and then, without warning, he dropped to his knees before me. Resting back on his haunches, he looked up at me adoringly. Laughter escaped me and his eyes twinkled as I reached out and instinctively put my hand on his head. I could almost feel him urging me on. Something certainly was, and I was getting high on the rush it delivered. After I stroked his head, he rubbed it against my thighs in an affectionate, catlike way, first one side, than the other. It was an incredibly sensual thing to do and my pussy was getting hotter and damper all the time. Arousal and self-awareness of the observers affected me strangely. I couldn't quite believe it, and for some reason I couldn't stop smiling. It was different from what I had thought it would be, though, because it felt so ... right. Something inside of me was responding to him, and it felt good.

"You're diverting attention from the band," I teased, when he stood up, speaking close against his head so he could hear me.

"Ah, but they don't mind, they're friends." He looked toward the stage and as he did I realized the singer had been watching him and she was beaming. She winked at me. I felt welcomed, part of it, and oddly at home.

Daniel reached inside his leather jacket again, his hand resting there. *What would it be this time?* I wondered with anticipation.

From the pocket, he pulled out a whip, a cat-o'-nine-tails with its leather strands wound tight around the handle. *A whip.* I watched as he ran the strands through his fingers, untangling them. My heart was pounding. I couldn't imagine where the situation was going next. Just thinking about it set me on a roller coaster of emotions. Over his shoulder, I saw that several members of the audience were completely riveted. Men. Hungry men, with envy in their eyes. Did they think we were together? That we were part of the show?

Before I had time to wonder any more, the singer jumped from the stage and strode toward us as she belted out the lyrics of her song. She took the whip from Daniel and pointed it at the ground. I watched, riveted, as he knelt and curled over. Moving to the music, she thrashed his upper body through his leather jacket. As he pulled the jacket tight I became aware that there was something under it. Daniel was wearing a bondage harness under his clothes. My pussy clenched.

The singer handed me the whip and smiled, before leaping back onto the stage. She hovered at our side of the stage, where the light poured down onto us. There was a moment of fear, a moment of confusion, and then it happened: A rampant urge to do it, to take control, rose up inside me, as if a switch had been tripped. I knew what to do, and why. I stepped over to where he was crouching, looking up at me with expectation. I clenched the handle of the whip, running the strands of leather across my other hand. What would it feel like, whipping a man? My body told me how it would feel: good. Any doubt I had was pushed aside as I reminded myself that he wanted it, and he enjoyed this. So would I.

The audience had created a semicircle around him, and I stepped in front of them, facing the stage. Music pounded in my ears, powering me up even more. My senses were being overloaded, and yet I was strangely honed and clear-headed. I was in this scene. More than that, I was in control of it now.

Oh God, how good it felt. I was wet, my sex clenching.

I ran the strands of leather across his back, testing it out. The line of his bondage harness was obvious now. As I considered how it might feel for him, and for me, something flared inside me: need, and desire. I thrashed him across the back of one shoulder, then the other, moving in rhythmic patterns. He flinched at each thrash and my pussy gushed. The rush of power I got, heady and deviant, startled me with its intensity. Pleasure ripped through me. I bent down and put my hand under his jacket and T-shirt, grasping for the harness. Pushing my fingers under it, I gripped, applying enough tension so that he would feel it all over his body.

His hands went to the floor, bracing himself, and I knew I had tuned into something. "You naughty boy," I said with delight against his head.

Shame poured out of him.

I lifted and stepped away from him, returning to my pillar at the stage, the whip dangling from my hand. My heart was pounding. I couldn't believe what I'd just done and, most of all, I couldn't believe the way it made me feel. Daniel rose to his hands and knees and padded over to me, like a pet panther. He stayed by my feet for the rest of the gig, his head rubbing against me affectionately. As I stroked his head in between taking photographs of the band onstage, a feeling of inner calm washed over me. Even though I was still aroused, startled, and confused by my reaction, it was like a feeling of honesty and true realization.

This has empowered me.

The whole experience had been like sex itself, with its arousal, its peak, its transcendence. I'd had no clue I would enjoy dominating a man, whipping him publicly, but I had. And, judging from the adoration at my feet, it was a two-way street.

As the gig ended, the lights went up and everyone was suddenly far too real for me. I didn't want the staring eyes anymore. I needed a drink. I needed space to think through what had happened to me. The band members were with Daniel; he was on his feet, chatting. Maybe if he hadn't been with me, he would have gone to someone else. Whatever his reason for choosing me to approach, it had altered my life. Grabbing my stuff, I headed to the bar downstairs, where I ordered a double shot and downed it quickly. My legs were like jelly as I put down the glass and made ready to leave. Daniel was on his way down the stairs, and the mask was gone.

I wanted to go home and think about it, savor the strange sense of euphoria that had overcome me back there. But if I left now, would I ever see him again? Unsure how far I wanted to go along this path, I headed for the door and out into the street. It had rained and the street was different from when I had gone inside. So was I. I ran up the hill, passing underneath the railway arches toward the station. When I heard his footsteps echoing under the arches behind me, I knew it was him. I stopped and turned back to look at him.

He held up his hands in a sign of peace. "I wasn't going to come after you, but something made me."

I nodded. I wasn't afraid of him; I realized it was me that I was afraid of. The unknown me who had risen up so quickly, so unexpectedly. My inner vixen, as I would later identify her.

"You were so good," he whispered and reached to stroke my arm affectionately.

"Why did you come over to me?"

"I could tell you wanted to play. You did, didn't you?"

He was right, but he had known and I hadn't. That was unnerving. He was still stroking my arms. I noticed that we felt like equals now. In fact, his seductive movement against my skin felt as if he was taking charge of me. Uncertainty reigned. "I have to go."

"Don't go. Don't deny it." He smiled hopefully, but I saw a flicker of regret in his eyes. He thought I was leaving.

"I've never done this before," I confessed, needing him to know that.

He stared at me, and then after a moment he stepped closer, that mischievous smile of his surfacing. With his hands around my upper arms I felt strangely secure, and yet curious and aching for more. A complete stranger had this effect on me? It was because he recognized his opposite in me. The thought crossed my mind, and I didn't reject it.

"Did you want to do it again? Did you want to do more? Somewhere private, perhaps?"

Images flashed through my mind, images brought on by that suggestion, images of fantasies I hadn't ever recognized that I had, but were suddenly growing fast and multiplying in my mind, assailing me with their erotic potential, their absolute promise of pleasure.

"Maybe," I murmured.

We stood there in the gloom of the damp tunnel, with the sound of cars driving down the rainy streets surrounding us. There was no need to say more. When his head dipped and his lips brushed over mine, my inner vixen whispered to me: *Don't turn away.*

I didn't.

I couldn't.

And so here we are, months later, and I am so glad I didn't turn away that night. Reaching down, I unbind him before I grab the whip. The mark of my heel on his back is like the center of a bull's-eye. I use it to focus me, because whipping him gives me such a rush that I need that anchor. When I'm done and he's shuddering with need, I step in front of him.

His forehead rests against my pussy. "Thank you, Mistress."

I feel his breath on my skin, the brush of his forehead across my naked mons. I want him to fill me, physically, as he has filled me emotionally and spiritually. "Lie down," I instruct.

He rolls onto his back, opening his fly, knowing what I want, never once breaking eye contact with me. His cock bounces free, long and hard, oozing. Climbing over him, I lift and lower, taking him inside, my sex hungrily eating him up while my boots bite into his flanks. Looking down at him, I know that what Daniel saw in me may never have been revealed by anyone else, and that makes me snatch at him, my nails driving into his shoulders as I grind down onto his cock. He recognized her in me before I did. He told me he could see her, showing me the real me.

I make love to him fast and hard. Taking him, using him, devouring everything he gives, until his body bucks up under me. He spurts inside me and then I come, with loud and determined force, reveling in the sense of power and release. The inner vixen, risen and reigning supreme.

VICTORIA'S HAND

Lisette Ashton

London, England, 1890

The parlour was quiet enough so Victoria could hear the tick of the grandfather clock from the hall outside. Stark spring sunlight filtered through the net curtains to illuminate the elegant furnishings. The family's finest bone china was laid out on a lily-white tablecloth. The afternoon tea was completed with freshly baked French fancies. Sitting comfortably in one of the parlour's high-backed chairs, Victoria placed one lace-gloved hand over the other, adjusted her voluminous skirts, and stared down at Algernon as he knelt before her.

She knew what was coming.

She had anticipated this day for months.

Before he started to speak, she knew what he was going to say.

It was the first time they had ever been together without a chaperone. Unless he had come to the house with this specific purpose, her parents would not have allowed her to spend any time alone with a suitor. The idea of her being alone with a man was simply too scandalous for civilised society to contemplate.

"Victoria, my dearest," he began.

There was a tremor of doubt in his voice. Victoria liked that. It suggested that he wasn't entirely certain that she would say yes. His bushy moustache bristled with obvious apprehension. His Adam's apple quivered nervously above his small, tied cravat. His large dark eyes stared up at her with blatant admiration. He looked as though his entire future happiness rested on her response to this single question.

She was dizzied by the rush of rising power.

"I've spoken to your father," Algernon began. "I've discussed the matter with my own parents and employer. I've even gained tacit approval from the local bishop. But now comes the time for the most important response of all, my dearest. Victoria: I've come to ask for your hand."

She smiled smugly to herself.

Outwardly her face remained an impassive mask.

"Algernon," she murmured. "I don't know what to say."

"Say yes," he replied quickly.

She allowed her lips to twist into a demure smile.

He fumbled in the pocket of his waistcoat and produced a small, gilt-edged box. Almost dropping it in his haste, he snapped the lid open and showed her a quaint ring that was encrusted with microscopically small semiprecious stones. She recognised it as one of the "DEAREST" rings that were currently enjoying popularity. The initial letter of each stone—a diamond, an emerald, an amethyst, a ruby, another emerald, a sapphire, and a topaz—spelt out the word "dearest." The eclectic collection of colours made Victoria think it looked more like a childish novelty than a genuine declaration of their betrothal.

"This is a mere token of our betrothal," he gasped.

"Yes," Victoria agreed. She made no attempt to take the

offered jewellery. "It is a mere token. With heavy emphasis on the word 'mere,' I think."

He blinked with surprise.

She could see it was time to test his mettle. Straightening her back, quietly deciding she liked having Algernon on his knees before her, Victoria said, "Do you want me to consider you as a potential husband?"

"I'd be honoured."

"Then get your cock out. Let me see what I'd be getting."

The words hung between them like a thrown gauntlet. The clock in the hall outside continued to tick loudly. Algernon studied her face with an expression that was almost comical. "Victoria?" he whispered meekly. "I don't think I heard you correctly. Could you please forgive me and say that again?"

"Get your cock out," Victoria said flatly. "If I'm going to consider marrying you, I want to make sure you're carrying something more impressive than that crappy little ring you just offered me."

His cheeks flushed bright pink.

She could feel the inner muscles of her sex clutching as she watched him squirm. His embarrassment and awkwardness were exhilarating to behold. Knowing she had inspired those responses made her moist along the line of her pussy lips. "If you want me as a wife, I have every right to know what my husband will be bringing to the marital bedroom. Get your cock out and show me the goods, or I'll have one of the servants escort you out of here now."

Again he hesitated. It took all of Victoria's restraint not to rub her thighs together and gleefully enjoy his dilemma. Inside the tightly laced bodice of her corset, her nipples were hard and aching. A wave of light-headedness came close to making her swoon in the high-backed chair where she waited.

"Unbutton your pants. Show me your cock. Or go away and tell your parents, your employer, and the bishop that I've rejected your offer. The choice is yours, Algernon. But make it quickly. The tea is cooling."

He began to fumble with the buttons at the front of his trousers.

The ring box fell to the floor and the gaudy jewellery dropped, forgotten, on the Oriental rug. Algernon's face was the shade of flustered crimson that Victoria had seen on the angered cheeks of drunks and brawlers. On his bookish face the colour was surprisingly fetching. She lowered her gaze as soon as he had exposed himself. The flaccid tube of his pink flesh hung innocuously from the front of his pants.

"It's not very big, is it?" she sneered.

"It gets bigger," he said defensively.

"Then make it bigger," she snapped. "Because at the moment, that appalling little engagement ring looks slightly more attractive."

For an instant she thought he might refuse. If there was any point when he was likely to reject her authority, Victoria knew it would be this moment, when she had insulted both his gift and his manhood. To make sure he didn't take advantage of the opportunity and go scurrying back to the sanctuary of his friends and family, she tugged the frills of her skirt up and dared to reveal a stocking-clad ankle.

"Make it big enough," she coaxed, "and I might consider saying yes."

He began to pull on himself.

His gaze was fixed on her ankles and his concentration appeared hard enough to etch wrought-iron. His hand moved quickly up and down the limp length of his cock and she watched the meagre tube of flesh thicken and grow. His fist was tight around the shaft, trapping blood into the dark and bulbous dome. As his hand continued to work, she saw that his fist had to travel further each time to go from the base to the end.

"Stop masturbating," she snapped.

He obeyed instantaneously.

She grinned at the eager way he had given himself over to her control.

"It's an adequate length," she conceded. She hoped that her smile was not so wide that he would realise she wanted him. If she was to accept his offer of marriage, this was a vital moment in their relationship. If she could make Algernon understand from this moment onward that she was the one in control, he would be her malleable slave for the rest of their days together. "Do you know how to use that cock of yours?"

"I … I think I know wh-what to do with it," he stammered.

"You may carry on handling yourself while we discuss my terms to accepting your offer," she declared haughtily.

Automatically, Algernon's hand went back to his cock. He stroked himself slowly and eventually managed to tear his gaze from her ankles so he could study her face. Certain that he would be more easily controlled if he wasn't studying her eyes, Victoria inched her skirts higher. She was showing off her shins, and felt silently proud that she had elected to wear her sheerest stockings today. As she pulled the skirts higher, Algernon stroked himself more swiftly.

"Are you attached to that moustache?"

He floundered. "It grows from my face," he said, sounding puzzled. "Is that what you meant?"

"No, Al-ger-non." She recited his name with the impatience of a disappointed schoolmistress. "You know perfectly well that's not what I meant. I was asking if you would lose that moustache if it meant I would consent to being your wife." She hitched her skirts higher. It was a daring pose that revealed her knees. Another few inches and he would be able to see the tops of her stockings and the alabaster flesh of her thighs.

"Don't you like the look of my moustache?"

"It's not the look that worries me," Victoria purred. "I'm more concerned about the way it will feel when you lick my pussy."

He held himself rigid.

She understood that he was on the verge of climaxing and admired the restraint he showed in holding off his potential orgasm. His eyes were momentarily glazed. His mouth hung open as though he had almost pulled too hard and pushed himself beyond the brink of reasonable self-control. Delighted by his torment, Victoria lifted her skirts still higher.

Algernon's gaze fell to the tops of her stockings. She could see his eyes widen as he noted the pale flesh of her upper thighs. He licked his lips with appreciation when he saw the thatch of curls that covered her most intimate secrets.

Aside from selecting her finest hosiery for this appointment, Victoria had elected to meet Algernon without donning any undergarments. It was a bold way for a young lady to deport herself, but she now understood that her courage was reaping ample rewards. "Should we see how your moustache feels against me?" she suggested. "A young lady has a right to know about these things before making a commitment of this magnitude. Would you care to tongue my hole for a moment so I can decide whether or not you may keep your moustache?"

He nodded.

She sensed that his excitement was so great that he couldn't properly articulate his desire to do as she had asked. Still stroking his length, and shuffling awkwardly forward on his knees, he lowered his face toward her sex.

Victoria held her breath as his tongue squirmed closer. A part of her wanted to judiciously concentrate on the pleasure he was able to bestow. She wanted to fairly gauge the sensation of having his prickly moustache so close to the tender flesh of her sex. She was struggling hard to be the dominant member of their burgeoning relationship and wanted to behave in the manner she thought most befitting an authoritative young lady.

But arousal constantly distracted her thoughts.

A soft tongue was lapping at the outer lips of her sex.

She arched her back against the seat.

The warmth of Algernon's breath proved maddeningly exciting. He teased the dewy lips of her cleft until she felt almost dizzy with the need for climax. She could tell he was positioning himself carefully, trying not to brush her most sensitive skin with the abrasive tickle of his bushy moustache. Occasionally an errant hair scoured her flesh, but it was a small distraction compared to the bliss of his tongue travelling over her pussy. Nevertheless, she could see that the facial hair might eventually present a problem.

"My clit," she insisted. "Tongue my clit."

It was a test. If he understood what she meant, and went on to find her clitoris, she would consider taking him as her husband. If he pulled back and looked puzzled, she would push him away and tell him he was unworthy.

Algernon's tongue slipped to the top of her sex and stroked the pulsing bud of her arousal. The sensation was enough to make her groan. Victoria stuffed the back of her hand against her mouth to stifle a scream of delight. She pressed her shoulders back against the chair and thrust her pelvis sharply toward him. The urge for release had been strong before; but now, as his tongue chased lazy circles against the throbbing bead of her clitoris, she realised she was only moments away from ecstasy. Knowing she had to show some restraint, determined that Algernon would not reduce her to a quivering wreck of satisfaction, Victoria steeled herself against the pleasure and said, "Now, tongue inside my hole."

He was more obedient than she had dared to hope.

The tongue slid slowly from her clitoris and eased itself between her labia. The warmth was divine. The intimate penetration felt so intense that Victoria had to grip the arms of the chair to maintain her show of equanimity. His tongue slid deeper, transporting her to a plateau of unparalleled delight. And then she was cresting a cloud of satisfaction so strong that she couldn't hold herself back. Her inner muscles went into a joy-inspired convulsion. The fluid heat of her sex grew so hot that she was momentarily seared by its brilliance. The shock of pleasure was so strong she wanted to scream with jubilation.

With a magnificent show of control, Victoria remained composed throughout the climax. Muted tremors shook her body but she wouldn't allow Algernon to see how strongly they affected her disposition. Pushing his face away, she adjusted her skirts and easily regained her previous composure as she settled herself decorously in the parlour's high-backed chair.

"That was pleasantly done," she allowed. Glancing down at him, she saw that his fist remained clutched around his thick length. The idea of having him thrust between her legs was suddenly so appealing that it almost overwhelmed her. He had teased her sex to a wet and wanton furnace, and she could imagine him stoking those fires further as he rammed into her, again and again. With an amazing show of self-discipline, Victoria pushed that thought from her mind and regarded him coolly. "Continue doing that while you admire me," she declared. "And I will set out the terms and conditions that you need to meet before I consent to be your wife."

He nodded eagerly. His hand slid slowly along his throbbing shaft.

"First," she said. "If you want me to be your wife, you'll provide me with a far better engagement ring than the piece of crap you offered before."

He nodded and apologised.

She spoke over him. "Diamonds," she explained. "Large ones are best. And I think they always sit more prettily in white gold. Second, and this is vital if you ever want to taste my pussy again: Lose that bloody moustache."

"Of course." He started to tell her it would be shaved off before the end of the day, but she was talking over him.

"Third—and this is most important of all—I want you to know that I'm in charge of our relationship. You may go to the races, and the gentlemen's clubs. You may pursue your career as best befits a gentleman of our times. But when you arrive at home, you will get down on your knees when I tell you, and you'll obey every instruction I give. Do you understand and accept that condition, Algernon?"

Victoria could see the hesitancy on his face. She watched his resistance flicker and die. She adjusted her voluminous skirts, giving him a brief flash of the sodden pussy lips he had just tasted, and knew he was won over by the sight.

"I understand and accept," he panted. "You shall be in control of our relationship."

Her smile was thin-lipped with satisfaction. She gestured for him to come closer and said, "Very well. You may leave shortly and go and tell your parents, your employer, and the bishop that I have consented to be your wife." Her gaze sparkled with mischievous intent as she reached for his length. Encircling his shaft with lace-gloved fingers, she said, "But before you go and do any of those things, didn't you say you wanted my hand?"

MARK OF OWNERSHIP

Teresa Noelle Roberts

I laid out my instruments with care: Wrist and ankle cuffs. Rubbing alcohol and cotton balls. Latex gloves. Scalpel from a medical supply store, still in its sterile package but gleaming menacingly under the bright light. Earlier, we'd had the lights low in the spare bedroom I used as a playroom while we'd fooled around and I'd flogged him—it disguised the fact that the conversion from spare room to dungeon was a work in progress—but after we took a break for pizza, I'd turned up the light for the next stage of our play.

And not just for the cutting. I wanted to be able to see every nuance of expression on Ben's face, the slight widening of his eyes as he looked at my tools, the movement of his Adam's apple as he gulped.

The way his cock jumped to attention, not quite hard at the thought of what was to come, but definitely getting there.

I reached out, cupped his balls, watched his cock finish growing thick and rigid and purple-black. Beautiful.

This wouldn't be the first time I'd drawn Ben's blood. We'd done needle play a couple of times, starting with one simple play piercing and working up to a fairly elaborate design, laced with colored ribbon, circling his nipples. Each time, I'd been left almost as shaken as he was, riding an endorphin rush of my own and flying so high that it was hard for me to pull myself back to self-control and guide his flight home. It wasn't the blood itself, although the effect of the ruby droplets against his chocolate skin was mesmerizing. It was the rush of absolute power, that someone would lie down and let me open the envelope of his skin.

Absolute power on my side, absolute trust on his, for those moments.

I'd never cut him before, but we'd talked about it, excitedly, almost obsessively.

It was as close as we ever came to talking about love.

"You know what's coming," I said, and he nodded. "Do you want it?"

He nodded again, but I needed to hear an actual word, spoken consent, so I asked again.

This time he answered, "Yes, Lady." As always when he was excited but nervous, the sweet notes of his West Indian childhood slipped into his voice. "Please."

He was the only person who'd ever called me Lady. Ma'am, Mistress, the occasional ironic Angel (because my name is Angelique), but never Lady.

I'd miss that.

We'd figured out almost as soon as we'd started dating that we were madly compatible sexually, but not so much in other ways. He's an ethical vegan (I'd had to invest in new rubber floggers just for him); if Carnivore were a religion, it would be mine. He's a perky morning person; I prefer to work third shift. I like night clubs that play industrial music; he'd rather do something outdoors where there are bugs and UV rays and various other nasties I'd like to avoid. I'm urban to the core; he was tired of city life. He ultimately wanted to settle down and start a family; I'm not opposed to monogamy (in theory and in the future), but kids are out. About the only thing we had in common was my need to control and his to surrender. So we'd agreed from the start—even while he yielded sexually, to a degree that surprised both of us almost as much as it turned us on—that we could both date other people while we enjoyed the wild ride.

Perhaps inevitably, that wild ride was drawing to an end.

Ben was getting more and more serious about his other lover, a smart, funny, woman who could actually share a meal with him and sleep on the same schedule he did and stuff like that— the things that make it possible to build a life together, not just a sex life. She wanted kids someday. She wasn't bone-deep kinky to the degree Ben and I were, but she was adventurous, willing to experiment. He hadn't said anything conclusive yet about leaving, but we both knew it was just a matter of time before he and Jasmine decided that the logical next step was monogamy. Every time we'd seen each other lately, there'd been that edge of desperation in our play, half trying to hold on to each other, half trying to tear each other apart, that you get when something's ending and you know you have to let it.

And mostly I was all right with that. I'd miss Ben—okay, I'd miss him a *lot,* his sweet yielding, his lovely body, his innate gentleness that balanced my sharp edges—but I'd always known I was a detour on Ben's path. I'd like to think I was a scenic detour with breathtaking vistas, but a detour nevertheless. I'd met Jasmine, and I approved. She'd take good care of his heart and soul, better than I could, and I saw a core of steel in her that suggested she could learn to take care of his body the way he needed, as well.

The part of me that was civilized and mature and that cared about Ben's well-being was all good with Jasmine.

The part of me that put a collar on him was growling in the darkness, snarling, *Mine, mine, mine,* and wanting to hold on with teeth and claws and not let go, not even if he tore himself apart struggling.

And I cared too much for him to let that happen. I didn't love him in a want-to-spend-the-rest-of-my-life-with-him way like Jasmine seemed to, but I did love him. He'd given himself to me. Now it was time to return him to himself.

So this was our last date, and after this I'd be the one to end things. With his personality and the dynamic of our relationship, he probably wouldn't be able to make the break, even though he obviously needed it. He'd wait for Jasmine or me to raise the issue, and Jasmine wasn't ready to issue an ultimatum yet, so I was going to have to be the bad guy. Girl. Whatever.

But first I wanted to give him something to remember me by.

I stood on my tiptoes to kiss him, felt him against me, hard all over, but melting into me as if he really was made of sweet, dark chocolate, softening against the heat of my skin.

My cunt throbbed, knowing that this beautiful, strong man was mine to do what I pleased with. Not for much longer, but my cunt didn't care about that. Cunts only think about *now, baby, now.*

I rubbed myself against his cock, feeling my juices flowing and slicking him, earlier in the game than they normally would. I'd been thinking about tonight all day, thinking through what I wanted to do to him, how I'd make this night memorable, and now, even though we'd fucked before dinner, I was almost shaking with lust from merely thinking about what I was about to do.

I was tempted to push him down, right onto the floor, and ride him until we were both sweat-slicked and spent, clawing at him with my nails, biting him until I left purple marks on his dark skin, urging him to do the same for me because even though I'm not into pain the way Ben is, sometimes that rough edge feels really good.

If we did that, though, I'd be too spent to carry out my plans, and we were both looking forward to it way too much for that. But I did need something. I put one of his big hands on my breast, pushed another between my legs, and hissed, "Make me come now or I'll be too distracted."

He obeyed, of course. He was extremely obedient.

And very good with his fingers, and strong enough to lift me onto the bondage table so he could get better access, and quite happy to kneel in front of me to finish the job.

Dreads tickling my pale thighs, tongue tickling my clit, fingers opening me, pleasure pulsing out, hot and sweet and building swiftly. Urgent, but at the same time soft and melting, making my body feel languid except for my cunt and belly, where glorious tension was growing with each lick, each thrust of his fingers.

I could just order him to stay with me, I thought—to use the word *thought* very loosely. It was more a series of scattered sexy images than an actual coherent thought: Ben as a slave boy from an erotic novel, naked, collared, and bejeweled, kneeling to await my pleasure.

My cunt jumped.

My boy. Soon to be marked. Ruby collar, ruby droplets on his skin.

He must have felt my body tightening, getting ready to explode, because he sped up his thrusting fingers and flicked his tongue in a way that he knew made me crazy, and I shattered, clenching around his fingers, driving my nails into his skin, and hissing, "Mine."

He breathed, "Yours, Lady," into my sopping pussy, and for

a few seconds the specter of Jasmine didn't stand between us.

I purred, licked my juices off his face, and slipped down to my feet.

"Lie facedown," I ordered, gesturing at the table I'd just vacated. He did, making himself as comfortable as possible while I put the cuffs on his wrists and ankles and secured them to the rings on the table.

For a few seconds, maybe longer, I gazed at him, enjoying the view, memorizing the lines of his body.

Not the only man in my life, but definitely the hottest. Jasmine was a lucky girl. And hell, so was I, even if I was feeling a bit wistful at the moment.

I drew a deep breath, cleared my mind of everything except Ben and me.

I ran my hands down the broad muscles of his back and the fine curves of his ass until he sighed and stirred like a great cat.

I cupped his ass in my hands, kneading, gripping, worrying at the tender spots from the earlier flogging. Even fastened down, he had some play of motion, and he pushed his butt up toward me, encouraging me.

Bad boy. He knew I liked to take things at my own pace.

I smacked his ass, as if that was going to discourage him. He rolled his hips, and it was so pretty that I deviated from my plan and gave him a light spanking, giving a darker flush to his skin as the blood rose. More warm-up than I'd meant to give, but I liked hearing the change in his breathing, liked feeling the warm resilience of his muscular butt under my hand.

Liked it enough that the warm, languid feeling spread throughout my body again, and I could feel my nipples, which had started to relax, getting perky once more.

Then I turned from him and prepared, making sure he heard a snap as I pulled the gloves on. I took the scalpel out of its packaging, leaving the safety cap on, and walked the cool of it over the heated skin of his ass. Then I slipped the safety cap off and carefully ran the flat against him, practicing the movements I'd need to make.

I could see his skin respond: goosebumps, and a sense that while he was holding himself very still, all the small muscles just below the surface were twitching. So hot.

"Are you ready, Ben?" I asked, already knowing how he'd answer.

"Oh God, yes."

"I could just tease you like this for hours. Threatening, never actually cutting. Maybe that would be better. No blood, no marks, just torment."

"Please, Lady. Don't make me wait any longer."

I let him feel the dull edge of the blade, a taste of what would come. He made a noise deep in his throat that barely sounded human. He was gone, on his way to the cosmic place where subs go when things get really good.

"But you'll have to wait a little while longer." I turned, breaking contact at the last possible minute, and got the alcohol and cotton balls.

He winced at the cold touch, the medicinal smell. His skin twitched. And then he sighed and made a begging noise, a ridiculously, beautifully small noise from that big body.

My heart was racing with excitement, and I was glad I'd just come. Otherwise, I'd have been shaking from the pent-up tension, and that couldn't have been good under the circumstances. As it was, his reactions were hitting me right between the legs, causing a small, steady pulse in my clit.

A little alcohol on the blade (I know it came out of a sterile package, but extra care did no harm), and then I was as ready as I'd ever be.

The first line didn't actually break skin; I erred on the side of caution. Just a line, white against his darkness, but he reacted violently—a shudder and a sobbing noise that I knew was pleasure but might not have sounded that way to someone who hadn't walked this road with him before.

I tried again, tracing that same line a little harder. For a second, nothing happened and I thought I'd once again been too gentle. Then, like a paper cut, it began to ooze a fine red line.

I let out a breath I hadn't realized I was holding and said, "You're bleeding, Ben, and it's lovely. Just lovely."

And he let out a breath I'd definitely realized he was holding, because sometimes you're more aware of your sub's body than your own, and said, "Thank you, Lady."

"More?"

"Please."

I poised the blade, lightly traced the line I would need to make—didn't want to make an error—then cut. This time my hand felt a little more confident, a little steadier, and I echoed Ben's sound of pained pleasure with one of my own.

More blood, and an upside-down *V* standing out, red, on his ass. Most of me was right there, holding the cool scalpel in my hand, focused on Ben, but some small part of me was floating around the ceiling on a good endorphin rush from the power and the beauty of it all. And if *I* was, I could only imagine how blissed-out Ben must be.

"One more," I said. "Can you come for me when I do it?"

He answered by writhing his hips against the table, giving himself a little more stimulation. I reached with my free hand, fondled his balls, which twitched and tightened, pulling in as his arousal grew; teased at his anus, which puckered and winked at me, hoping for more attention. He gasped and pushed against me as best he could, and for a while I indulged us both. Once his breathing seemed ragged enough, his balls taut enough, I kissed the back of his neck and went back to business.

"Beautiful Ben," I whispered. "Beautiful, beautiful Ben. Hold still." I pressed the tip of the scalpel against him, and he froze. "I'm going to cut you now."

One more fine line of red bloomed in the blade's wake.

"Do you know what this is, Ben? It's an A, my initial. Come for me now."

And he did, so hard I had to jerk my hand back so he didn't run my good work by cutting himself accidentally as he thrashed.

Once I thought his legs would support him, I helped him up and took him to the mirror so he could see his monogrammed butt. It wasn't very big or very deep. Within a few days—before the weekend, when he'd be going to see Jasmine again—it would heal, perhaps leaving a fine scar that would fade to invisibility in time. But he'd know it had been there.

At first his face was dazed, excited, proud—all the lovely things you expect to see on a sub's face when he's just gone through a new experience and has a glorious new mark to show for it. Then he started to come down and a bit of worry slipped into his brown eyes. He reached behind him, touched the cuts lightly. "Does this mean … Jasmine … Did you want … ?" He couldn't quite get the question out, but I knew what he wanted to ask: Did this mean I wanted him to dump the woman he'd come to love?

"No, darling. Not in the least." I held him close, luxuriating in the feel of him against me, trying to ignore the tears that welled in my treacherous eyes. "You've belonged to me. I'd like to think a little bit of you always will, even if it's just a few square inches of your skin. But you belong with her, and we both know it. You're free, Ben, unless you really don't want to go. You'd just damn well better propose to Jasmine, oh, this weekend. And you'd better invite me to the wedding. My final orders."

I stopped breathing after I said that, hoping I'd read all the signs right and he'd been ready to move on, but not ready to say it. What if he broke down and started begging for me to keep him? I was strong enough to do what I was pretty sure was right, but if he gave me any reason to doubt it, all bets were off.

I didn't dare to look at his face until I heard him say, "Of course I will, Lady." I looked up then. He was crying and smiling, just like I was, and as I'd suspected, he seemed sad, but at the same time relieved that he hadn't had to say the words that needed saying. "Although I may need to wait a few weeks for the proposal, Lady. I'll need to find the right ring first."

"Angelique," I corrected. "If you'll have me as a friend." I was surprised how scared I was to ask that.

"Of course," he said, pulling me even closer, reminding me of his strength. "But I'll always think of you as Lady."

And, I thought, nestled against him, *I'll always think of you as mine, my own beautiful Ben.*

But when someone gives you the privilege of owning them, gives themselves to you as thoroughly as he had, they give you responsibilities with it.

And sometimes those responsibilities hurt far more than a thin surgical blade.

The cuts on his skin would heal quickly. The cut on my heart would take longer.

PINCH

Tara Alton

Six weeks ago, my friend Catherine was telling me about her dominatrix escapades during our smoking breaks at work. At first, we thought it was just between us girls, but we noticed a handsome man from the building eavesdropping. By the look in his eyes, we realized he could overhear our conversations. My learning what Catherine did to men had gotten my panties in a bunch more than once, so I wondered what it was doing to him.

Catherine had done all the light S/M stuff, from wrapping guys' dicks in cellophane to expertly whipping clothespins off their nipples with a crop to playing tic-tac-toe with ice cubes on their backs. She was now working her way into the heavy stuff. Her creativity made me feel like a schoolgirl who had done no more than the missionary position. Considering that I hadn't had sex for three years since my messy divorce, I could play the part. She had encouraged me to get into the "scene." I didn't have the nerve. I was pretty. My body was still in good shape at thirty-five years old, but I couldn't imagine myself the exotic temptress who wore high heels and leather and who dominated men.

But that all changed the day that Catherine excused herself to get an iced tea before returning to our desks. I headed to the elevator alone. The man from our breaks followed me. Once the elevator door closed and we hit our respective floor buttons, I looked at him. I was surprised by what I saw. I had never looked at him that closely, but I guessed he was near my age and around 5'9". Now I took in the details of his dark hair, untouched by gray, and his brown eyes. He wore a gray suit with a rose-colored tie, and he smelled like strong coffee, cologne, and cigarettes.

A smile played at his lips as he caught me looking at him.

"I've been overhearing what you've been talking about with your girlfriend," he said. "It sounds very interesting."

I swallowed the lump in my throat. He had the type of voice that gave a woman a sexy chill, and the scent from his skin was making me a little heady. I moved a little nearer to him.

"Is this something you both do?" he asked.

He looked me in the eyes. My pussy gave a twitch.

"You should talk to Catherine about that," I said.

"And not you?"

"I'm not into that," I said.

"Maybe you're more into it than you thought. You seem to like it," he said. "I've seen the glimmer in your eyes as you listen."

Very calmly, he reached over to the STOP button on the elevator. The elevator lurched to a stop. My first impulse was to get away from him, but he took a step closer to me.

"It's not Catherine I'm interested in," he said. "It's you."

"I'm not a dominatrix," I said.

"It doesn't matter," he said. "You're the one I'm attracted to.

I want you to do something for me, and in return I'd be a very good boy."

A "very good boy" sounded like a line if I'd ever heard one, but I realized by the expression in his eyes that he was serious. He took my hand and gently pressed his lips to each knuckle. His lips were incredibly soft and warm. I found myself melting at his touch.

"So, you tell me what to do to you, and you submit to it?" I asked.

"Something like that," he said.

"It sounds more like you're controlling me," I said.

He didn't look up at me. Rather, he kept kissing my hand, and in between kisses, he spoke.

"Pinch me," he said.

"What?" I asked.

"Pinch."

He stopped what he was doing and pushed my shoulders to the wall of the elevator. His mouth was at my ear.

"Pinch me. My arms, my legs, my nipples, my skin, my ears," he said.

Taking my fingers, he pressed them to his earlobe.

"Tell me I'm a bad boy and I need to be punished. Give me a good pinch to make me behave."

He was so close to me that I could feel his breath getting shorter and the bulge beginning in his pants. Desire flashed in his eyes. He really wanted this. By the heat in my pussy, I knew I wanted it, too. I had been masturbating alone too long. So what if I was standing in an elevator about to commit a sexual act with a stranger? So what if it was a little kinky? With his earlobe between my fingertips, I pinched him hard. He gasped at the sudden pain, but he begged me to do it again.

I did. I tweaked his earlobes until they turned red. I worked my way down his chest, opening his shirt, running my fingers through his chest hair. I squeezed his nipples until they stood up as stiff as pencil erasers. It was delicious, telling him he was a very bad boy and how he had to hold very still.

His cock was clearly defined in his pants, and his breath was coming in gasps as I pulled his shirt all the way out of his pants and slid my fingers beneath the waistband.

Getting on my knees, I traced the outline of his hard cock with my fingertips, but I wasn't ready to go there yet. I pulled off his shoes and socks, and I pinched the tops of his feet and up his calves. As I brought my head up to cock level, I thought about the last time I had a cock in my mouth. I was dying for it. He started to undo his zipper, but I smacked his hand away.

"You're very bad," I said. "I think you need another pinch."

Sliding my hands in between his legs, I gave the inside of his thigh a good squeeze, enough to make his eyes water. He bit his lip. Slowly, I unbuttoned his pants, undid the zipper, and pulled down his underwear. His cock sprang forth. He was average length, but he was thick. I gave his cock a lick from the base of the shaft up to the top where my tongue lingered on his helmet head, feeling the texture.

I slid his cock into my mouth and sucked in my cheeks as I pulled in deeper. As I pulled his cock out, I gave the head a good flip with my tongue before I took it back in. Gripping my hair, he seemed to like it. I kept it up, taking more in each time until his cock was bumping the back of my throat. I wanted to reach down and play with my clit, which was aching with a steady pulse, but both my hands were occupied. One was stroking his shaft and one cupped his balls while I sucked him.

I tasted pre-come. I wanted to feel his cock get stiffer. I started to pick up the pace and lightly pinched the skin of his balls.

He sucked in his breath. Grabbing his hand, I made him hold himself while I pushed up my skirt and hooked my pantyhose and underwear with my thumb. Losing a beat only for a second, I got them down over my ass.

My finger slid into my naked pussy, getting my clit wetter. I made circles around it, keeping in time, meanwhile taking his gorgeous cock to the depths of my throat, making it mine.

The base of his cock started to tighten. He was going to come. So far gone in my blow job nirvana, I sucked furiously and pressed my clit harder. An orgasm built in my toes, collected itself. It rocked and rolled through my pussy, my legs and knees going weak.

"I'm coming," he said.

His thrusts into my mouth became shallow and quick. I heard him gasp. He fiercely came in my mouth. I felt each tiny throb as if it were a heartbeat.

After a few moments, I got to my feet, feeling a little shaky, but a lot better for the experience. I watched him adjusting his clothing and putting his socks and shoes back on. He didn't know it yet, but his earlobes had bruises as rosy as his tie. He pressed the START button on the elevator, as if he had done this a hundred times before, but as he got off on his floor, I reached out and gave his ass a good hard pinch.

Surprised, he turned and looked at me. With a satisfied glance, I knew I definitely was going to get off on this. There was another bulge in his pants.

"You promised to be a very good boy," I said. "I'll be waiting."

HIS JUST REWARDS

Rachel Kramer Bussel

"Hello?"

"Good, I'm glad you're home. I'm coming over in five minutes. Turn off your TV or computer or whatever else you have on. When I get there, I want you to be completely naked and ready for me. I'll let you know what to do when I get there. Okay?" I snap this out in my best commanding tone, never letting on that I'm shaking and nervous. I say this as if I talk this way all the time, even though so far I've only hinted at what a bitch I can be. I have a clear sense of direction and purpose, have summoned all my power for one final, explosive encounter that will only work if I play it cool.

I arrive a few minutes later and knock briskly on the door. He opens it naked but with sandals on. I march right in, pushing past him, pulling Karla into the room after me, daring him to ask me who she is or what she's doing here. Maybe he knows, maybe he doesn't, but it's not my problem.

"What are those doing on your feet?" I ask disdainfully,

pointing at the sandals. I don't wait for him to respond before continuing, "Take those things off and get down on your knees." Anticipating his protests about the dusty floor, I bark, "Don't argue, just do it!"

I hand Karla the bag and signal to her to fish out the riding crop I've packed specifically for this occasion. I feel much bigger than my 5'2" height, and not only because of the severe black heels I'm wearing. This is good, because he's big and strapping and I need all my willpower to go through with it. When he's on the floor, I nudge him with my foot, tapping his ass and telling him to start crawling. We follow him as he leads us to his office. "Now get up."

He keeps looking at me with those puppy-dog eyes that beg me to pet and kiss and coddle him, to give him a hint of the affection he's come to crave from me. But affection isn't a one-sided transaction, and I have only so much attention to give without getting what I require in return. I've been waiting for his side of the bargain, his compliance with my very simple demand, a question in search of an answer, and so far he hasn't come close. It's time to teach him a lesson.

He sits in the chair, and I secure his ankles to the chair's legs, then wrap bondage tape around his chest and knees, in enough places so that I'm confident that he's secured. I want to bind his wrists with rope but settle for only one, leaving the other free, not because I want him to use it, but to tempt him into committing acts I'll have to punish him for later. Karla senses that I don't need her help and goes off to the adjoining bedroom to wait for me.

"Even though I know you want to be the best little boy you can be and obey all my commands to the letter, I'm a little worried that you're going to try to talk to me or scream or make noise that will distract me from fucking Karla. So I'm just going to have to tape your mouth to prevent you from even attempting anything like that."

I pull off a length of the shiny red tape and fasten it over his mouth. I slap his cheeks lightly, one and then the other, and then, because it feels so good, again. His cheeks take on a rosy tone. "You look good like that. Don't you agree?" I ask in a babying tone as I pinch one cheek, hard. He nods, and I smile in response.

As I step back to survey my handiwork, he looks at me beseechingly. I bring my hand forward and caress his cheek. "Am I supposed to feel sorry for you, all alone out here with only a video to keep you company, turned around so you can't see us all naked and fucking each other? Have you ever seen two girls together? I bet you haven't, but the thought of it turns you on. I bet you'd like to watch, like to see her sucking on my nipples and me licking her pussy, like to see me lay her across my lap and spank her."

I look down and notice his cock twisting from his restrained lap, and I can't resist a brief stroke over his hardness. "Not that I know for sure what you're into, since you've been a bit reticent with that information, haven't you? But on this count I know I'm right. You *would* like that a lot, wouldn't you?"

He nods.

"Well, you'll just have to guess what we're doing, though if you're lucky you might get to hear her scream a little bit. But you're not gonna see any of it. I did bring this video to keep you company, and I selected it especially for you."

As I put the cassette in the VCR and queue it up, I'm reminded of my babysitting days, when a cartoon was all it took to pacify a screaming, whiny child. This video is for adults only, but I hope it will have the same effect. "Now, I'm going to get you settled in here and leave you with this video, and I want you to be good and quiet and pay attention. There'll be no stroking your cock. Like I said, I picked this video especially for you because I think there are some good lessons you can learn about what it means to be a good boy and respond to orders, and you'll see in it what happens when you don't. I want you to watch carefully what kinds of punishments these mean mistresses dish out, because that should give you a little taste of what's in store for you when I get back."

I watch as his eyes fixate on the image of a large man strung upside down from the ceiling of a dungeon, while two scantily clad, sexy women beat and torture him. A quick glance at his cock shows me that it at least is reacting positively to the images on the screen. I don't dare give away the fact that the video actresses are much stricter than I could ever be, even in my imagination, but that doesn't mean I can't try my best. I pull a clothespin out of my pocket and present it to him. "There's a reason I left your hand free, and it's not so you can play with your cock. It's for this. You can put it anywhere on your body that you want to, but when I come back I want to see it attached to you, *somewhere*. Otherwise I'll have the pleasure of clamping it somewhere very painful myself. Got that?"

I stand in front of him, blocking his view, daring him to try to twist to watch the TV around me, or otherwise stare right at my bulging breasts. My eyes bore into his, wondering if he can even appreciate the emotions underlying my actions. Yes, I know he's been craving some sort of abuse from me, but he's also pissed me off to the extreme. I have to watch myself that I don't go overboard, don't take too much of my anger out on his willing skin. The babysitting image returns when I think of how childishly he's been acting lately, wanting all the fun and none of the responsibilities of a real relationship. My questions go repeatedly unanswered, even though I find it hard to believe that a grown man doesn't have a response, can't articulate in words what gets him hard, what turns him on, what he wants. Women are supposed to be the mysterious, hard-to-read creatures, men as easy as saying, "Fuck me." But it doesn't actually work that way in the real world.

I wonder if I can hurt him enough that he'll give me the verbal contact that I crave, the communication that has been missing since the earliest days of our relationship. I wonder if there will come a day where I can ask him to spin me a fantasy, to let me into his head, even if only for a moment. Sadly, I don't think that's in the cards for us, so I'll take what I can get from him and move on.

"Now, watch your video like a good little boy. I'm not giving you a pen to take notes, but I hope you'll remember what you've seen because I'm gonna ask you about it. I'll be in the other room, but don't expect me back until I'm good and ready. And don't even *think* about trying to escape. When the video is over, you can sit there and play with your clothespin, but you're not to touch yourself and certainly not to come under any circumstance. Believe me, I'll know if you do. Got that?"

He nods again, and I walk away, filled with an energy that bursts through my whole body. I enter the bedroom and see Karla lying there, leafing through a magazine, and wonder if she's heard what exactly went on in the office. The sight of her fills me with an irresistible urge to touch her, taste her, to have her and never let her go. I forget any potential awkwardness over the fact that I've been naked in here with him, as well. Now it's only about me and her, nobody else. I have a brief urge to close the door, even though I know that there's no way he can come in here to watch. Anyway, it doesn't matter. Whenever I'm with her—whether we're in a private bedroom or on a public dance floor—it seems as if we're completely alone. I can melt into her, close my eyes, and all of a sudden the other people surrounding us disappear. We're the only ones in existence, and she's the only one occupying my attention.

The immature man I've just teased and taunted is nothing compared to her.

She glances up as I walk in, a slightly sheepish look on her face. Neither of us says anything, but a spark of understanding and desire fills the air. I pull her close to me and quickly undo her pants, then slide them down her thin legs. She's so small that sometimes I feel as if I'm with a doll, an otherworldly creature who is tender and delicate. And while she can be those things, she's shown me her strength and passion and vulnerability. I don't have to treat her like a soft flower.

"What have you been doing in here? Have you been good? Were you listening to what I said to him?"

She nods, a slightly contrite look on her face tinged with a hint of mischief. "Did you like that, Karla? Hmmm? Did you like the way I talked to him?" By now her pants are all the way off and I press the back of my hand against her panties, finding them wet and warm. "I think you did. I think you liked hearing me tease him and yell at him, didn't you?" I slide her panties to the side and stroke her, already so wet I want to plunge right in. Every time I touch her it's new and beautiful; I could get lost in her pussy and never return to the real world. I press more firmly, stroking only the outside of her wet slit even as I feel her pushing up against me.

"What was that, baby? Is there something you want from me? If there is, you're gonna have to tell me what it is. You should know that, especially after all I've been through with that one out there not letting me in on his secrets. I'll move closer so you can whisper in my ear." I pick her up and position her so she's across my lap face up, her face next to my ear and her pussy within arm's reach. I pull the panties completely off.

As much as I want to think that things with each of them are totally separate, that I've been conducting two equivalent relationships operating in separate spheres, inside, they have overlapped. The charge I got from tying him up, from knowing that I could do whatever I wanted to him, has bled over into my time with her. I'm surprised that after all these years of being told what to do, and liking it, the other side of the equation seems to fit me perfectly. My breathing quickens as she rubs up against me, her ass pressing into my lap and her face nuzzling my neck. I cup my hand over her pussy and leave it there, willing her to sit still. She does. The squirming stops and there is only silence and stillness, searching and sweet anticipation. I feel myself getting wetter as I realize that whatever is about to happen is under my control; I can go in whatever direction I want.

Just like that, with a split-second realization of power, I'm gushing. I push two fingers into her pussy, knowing that she's ready so I don't need to warn her. I press deeper and feel her arch up against me, her head lolling back as she tries to take me in and stay in control, but she can't. I push as far as I can go, then ease out of her. She grabs my wrist and tries to push me back inside her.

"Soon, baby, soon, don't worry," I whisper in her ear.

She whimpers and tosses her head back and it's a sight to behold, my Karla spread out before me as my personal plaything.

"Spread your legs for me, baby. There, that's good," I tell her as her legs widen and I can see all her pretty pinkness. I have no idea whether her other lovers talked to her like this. I am now getting used to figuring out what she wants and how I can give it to her.

I bring my hand upward and then down on her pussy, softly at first, then with my fingers I keep going—tap, tap, tap—against her, knocking lightly at first, then harder as I see that she likes it. As if something inside me has taken over, and I'm in a trance, I bring my hand back and forth again and again, gaining in intensity each time. I pause for a moment, afraid that I'm going to get swept away in my actions and hurt her, but she begs me to continue. I do, slapping her cunt and then once more slipping first two and then three fingers inside her, all with an urgency that we can both feel; I must fuck her right now or it will be too late. I push my fingers inside her, feeling for the most sensitive areas, pressing up and then to the side and almost wanting to cry with the magic of being so close to her center.

I let her lean back onto the bed and with my other hand press on her stomach and then slide lower, massaging her clit while pressing against her, covering her in my touch until she cries out and I feel her squeeze my fingers with a fierce intensity. I slowly pull out, awed by what has just happened, so fast and so furious. Awed but not shocked because it's like this every time we're together, with everything so new and raw and fresh I feel both like a wide-eyed virgin and like an old woman, full of power and wisdom. I pull her toward me and hold her, get lost in her for another spell of time as we recover.

When we finally emerge, I've lost track of time. I'm sure the video is long over. I wonder if he'll have his eyes closed, or be playing with his dick, or trying to escape. But when I come out, pulling a naked Karla along behind me, he's sitting there looking very angelic, his free hand dangling by his side, appearing so casual you'd think he could almost have strung himself up because he was bored.

"So, how was the video? Did it bore you? Is that why you're just sitting there? Where's the clothespin?" I say this louder than I need to, because I can, because I like the sound of my voice and want to startle him, and because I know that for once nobody is going to tell me to lower my voice.

He produces the clothespin with his free hand.

"Why didn't you put it somewhere? If I'd known you were going to not follow my instructions, again, I'd have tied up both your wrists."

His face reddens.

"What I think I'm gonna do is give it to Karla to put on you."

I slap his face for emphasis and present the pin to Karla. I know she won't do too much damage to him, thinking she'll try a finger or other easy spot, but she surprises me and zeroes in on his right nipple. I give him a look to silence any potential protests. There are so many delicious possibilities of what I can do with him now that I wonder how I'll manage to choose only one. I bend down and loosen his ankles from their bonds, knowing what I want, at least at this moment. With that extra bit of freedom, there has to be a tradeoff, and I secure his free arm behind his back since he won't be needing it right now. He looks up at me, a challenging expression on his face, as if he's ready to duel even though it's clear that with my ammunition I'll win easily. But since that's what he ultimately wants, I guess he wins, too. That kind of win/lose thinking is too confusing for me, so I shut everything else out of my mind except how this scene will end. It's the last time I'll see him, ever, so I have to make the most of it.

"I did that for a reason. Now, spread those legs for me. That's good," I say soothingly, buttering him up before I take him down. I raise the crop from the desk and hold it in my hand, surveying my subject. I still don't know if he understands why I'm really angry, but this isn't about my anger anymore, it's about something much deeper and darker than that. It's sad that we won't get to play like this again, but I don't have enough time to waste on immature men who think a top's job is to guess their fetish. I step forward so I'm again standing before him and lean down. I know he thinks I'm going to suck his cock, like I've done so many other times, but instead I go farther, licking my way along his thighs before sinking my teeth into his flesh. I bite without care for how it will feel for him, only knowing when to stop the moment I feel my teeth sink into tender skin, then keep going.

I pause, sucking on his thigh, wondering if this will give him a hickey. I continue on to the other thigh, and feel him try to thrash against the chair.

I stand and motion to Karla to come join me. She walks toward us and presses her naked body against my back. I reach behind me and fondle her wherever I can, wanting to kiss her and hold her, but knowing there'll be plenty of time for that later. For now, this brief contact will have to do. I lead her to a chair and have her sit and observe. Then I take the crop and slide its tip down his body, from his head down his cheek, over his chest, tapping it lightly against the clothespin for a moment before continuing. It reaches his cock and I see his arms jerk, trying to move forward to protect his precious jewels, but there's nothing he can do. I bat at him lightly, watch as his cock turns even pinker.

"Spread your legs wider," I instruct him, and he does. I raise the crop and then let loose, tapping and then hitting, harder and harder, along his inner thighs. He winces and tries to move, attempts to bring his legs together, but I work my knee between them, pressing gently against his balls as a reminder that I'm the one in charge. I continue this torment until I have the urge to form something stronger; I only have a little room to work with between his legs. I throw the crop onto the floor and straddle him, rubbing my pussy up and down along his cock. It feels good, no doubt, and for an instant I'm truly tempted to see what he would do with his cock if he could, but it's too late for that.

How many chances did he have to fuck me, and didn't? And

now he wants it, for some strange reason. I want to leave him
tied up here but sense that he needs something more. I get out
my pocket knife and swiftly slice through the bondage tape and
remaining ropes. I like the way the knife feels in my hand, the
implicit threat that I would never use, though he doesn't need to
know that. There's so much that he doesn't need to know, will
never know, now.

I push him roughly off the chair, and even though he out-
weighs me by a good eighty pounds, he staggers and has to catch
himself from falling off.

"Get up against the wall," I tell him, motioning where I want
him to go. While he positions himself, I get a few more imple-
ments out of my bag, holding the firm leather of the paddle in
my hand and feeling a calmness overtake me. I am about to
settle a score, make us both even, give him the beating he's been
secretly craving, fulfill the fantasy he's been too afraid to tell me
he wanted to do. And for that silence, ultimately, he will lose me.
Ironic, actually, but meant to be. I shake my head lest I stand
here too much longer regretting what might have been.

"Are you ready?"

"Yes, Miss," he says quietly. He's had enough time, perhaps
too much, to prepare himself. I close my eyes for a moment and
focus on what I want, then open them and step over to him. If I
were taller, I could simply lean forward and whisper in his ear,
but suddenly I'm glad I'm not. There's no need to pretend that
we share a false intimacy. This is simply a quid pro quo transaction that will give each of us something we've been craving, but
also leave both of us needing more.

"I'm going to spank you with this paddle, once for every year
of your age. You're going to count the strokes for me, and when
I'm done you're going to stand there until we leave. Do you understand?" I allow no emotion to enter my voice.

"Yes, Miss."

I start off sharp and strong, then ease off a little—not the usual way to do it, but this is a special occasion, the first and last time for this particular configuration, and I will do it my way. After ten strokes, I pause and place my hand over his reddened skin, kneading the warmth I feel there. With each squeeze, I feel him wriggle and I press my entire body up against his. I've chosen his age for the number of whacks as a symbol of all that he should know by now and doesn't, and also because I need a stopping point or we could be here forever. As I massage his ass, I know that there's a part of me that will regret leaving, despite all our differences; that will regret not going further. I wonder if it's my own fear, too, that has contributed to this détente, but even if it is, there's no going back. Before taking the next swing, I look over at the naked and sublime Karla, who is sitting and watching silently. I have no idea what she thinks, or whether she understands, but I hope that she does. I keep up a solid, even pace, with well-placed blows that land as harshly as I intended them. He tries not to make any noise, but I can hear the changes in his breathing, see the way his ass moves ever so slightly as it eagerly awaits my strokes. For the last three, I turn the paddle over so that the mean indentations on the other side—the one I've never dared use before—are facing him.

I step closer and say, "These last strokes are really going to hurt, so get ready." I say the words gently, tenderly, almost as if I want to protect him from myself, which in its own way is the truth. Suddenly, I want to step back, put the paddle down, leave. I don't know if I can finish the job, or if I care enough to expend the energy, but I must somehow, because after a deep breath I lift my arm again.

The three of us hear the loud SMACK as the paddle connects with his ass, and his hand hits the wall with a thud as he tries to process the pain. I don't let that stop me, and again repeat the motion on the other cheek. Before the final blow, the room is crackling with tension. Karla is standing now, staring, rapt as I take a quick glance at her and then back at him. He is tall, big, strong, and yet vulnerable here. I feel tears prick my eyes at how much I sense that he would give me, if only he knew how. I feel forgiveness settle into my body, knowing that he has not deliberately hurt me, only done the best that he could do. Alas, that was not enough for my needs, but maybe he will find someone for whom it will be.

I bring my arm back and release all the hurt, pride, honor, and forgiveness, and I almost feel it all leave me and enter him. The sound this time isn't quite as loud, but it leaves the room singing with its noise nonetheless. I want to say something, even if it's only "goodbye," but I can't. I press my hand against his back, letting my touch do the speaking for me, before quietly gathering my things. He leans his head against the wall, his eyes closed. Before we leave, I pull Karla close to me and we hug for a long minute. Then I grab our bag, let her dress, and take her hand as we go. We head to the park and sit on a bench and I lean my head on her shoulder, and we sit for a long time. Maybe I was wrong. Maybe there are some things that can be said without words, with bodies and breath and movement. I lean over, bury my head in her neck, and she holds me. I don't even know what I feel—relief, sadness, hope perhaps. Whatever it is, words are not enough to convey it. I smile at that, knowing that he would understand perfectly.

WHY CAN'T I BE YOU?

Alison Tyler

Sounds silly, I guess, but sometimes when I see him, I don't want to fuck him, I want to *be* him. Matt has the perfect male body, in my opinion. Broad shoulders, a long, lean torso, slim hips, and an amazingly awesome ass. He has a deeply fuckable body, and I do love to fuck him. But sometimes I don't want him to climb on top of me and pound into me, don't want him to bend me over and take me from behind, don't want him to press me up against the wall and make me writhe with pleasure.

No, what I want is to slide inside him and see the world from within his head. And I want to devour some chicklet dolled up in one of those swishy floral dresses and tie-up espadrilles and fuck *her* while being him.

Too much like that John Malkovich movie?

Maybe.

But why can't I be him? Just for an evening. Or even for an hour. Why can't *I* be the one to move through the crowd and pick up a girl, any girl? (He can have any girl.) Why can't I take one home, or out to some back alley, and push her up against the brick wall out there, tear her panties down, and fuck her?

That's all I want. One hour. One hour inside of his body so that I can find out what it's like—not just to be a man, but to be *him*. I want to manhandle my throbbing cock, to hold it, to fondle it. I want to force-feed every inch of it to some pretty, summertime doll, to make her drink me, and drain me. To make her feel my power.

He's not always that type, I know. He is sweet and caring and gentle. He is monogamous and dedicated to me. But *I'd* be that type if I were him. I'd be the type to control the situation. I'd be the type to take charge. It would feel good to take charge. God, it would feel amazing.

My vision gets to a point where I am all-consumed by the thought. So I take one step forward, or really one roll forward on the mattress, and I curl my body up next to his in bed, and I say, "I have a fantasy …"

He slides one strong arm around me, holding me close. "Tell me, baby," he whispers back, the way he always does. He likes my mind best. More than my ripe, lush breasts. More than my thick, black hair. More than the curves of my hips or the swell of my ass, he likes my thoughts. My dirty fantasies. My X-rated visions. "Tell me where your mind is going tonight," he croons in his low, husky voice.

"I want …" I start, but I can't say it.

"Tell me."

"No," I whisper, shaking my head.

"Tell," he says, and his voice is insistent.

"I'll show you," I decide. Because that will work best.

"Show—" he starts, but I put my finger to his lips, and without another word, I climb out of bed and grab the satchel containing my outfit and all my recently purchased gear, and I disappear into our bathroom. I can almost hear his thoughts going crazy in the other room—*where is she going? What's she doing?*—but I pay more attention to my own thoughts. At this point, they're all that matter.

I gaze at myself as I bind my breasts flat with an Ace bandage. I admire my body as I slip into the recently purchased harness and adjust my fine, handsome cock. I slide into the faded 501s, and put on the boots, and add a wife-beater T-shirt that makes my arms look cut and fierce.

Who am I?

Will he know?

I gel my hair and tuck my ponytail up into a cap, then slip on a pair of his shades. I can see it. I can feel it. I add cologne, from the expensive bottle I bought him last Christmas, and then I walk back into our bedroom and wait to see what his response will be.

"Oh, Jesus," he sighs when he sees me, and I know with that ripple of pleasure that runs instantly through me that he's game. "Oh, *God*," he says, looking me up and down. I'm tall and lean and hard. My hand is already on my belt. I want to undress as quickly as I wanted to dress. But first, I have to strip him down. I have to oil him up. I have to kiss him all over, lovely flower that he is. Because now that I'm him, well, who does *he* have to be?

We don't need to answer that question, do we? I didn't think so.

Even though I feel like being naked so he can really see the transformation, I don't take off my clothes this time. I need him too fast for that. I part my jeans and let him admire my cock. I manhandle my cock, my fist wrapped tight. I want to slide it across his pretty lips. I want to watch him deep throat it.

He wants that, too.

"Look," I say. "Get close so you can see me. Really see me."

He scrambles on the bed to obey. His mouth is open before I can command it. I don't have to tell him what to do. His lips part, and he takes me in. I feel him pulling on my cock. I feel how hungry he is for that. I envision him draining me, taking me all the way to climax with the sucking motions of his ravenous mouth.

Later. *After.*

For now, I push him back. There's lube in the drawer by the bed. Usually, it's lube for me. Now, it's lube for him. I tell him to get me the bottle, and then I let him watch me grease myself up.

"You know where this is going," I say, seeing his eyes widen, seeing him bite hard on his bottom lip, as if he might want to say something, but doesn't quite dare. "You know," I say, softer, but I can tell from the rosy blush on his face that he understands. Of course he does. Then I roughly roll him over on the bed, and pull his boxers off, and spread those lovely asscheeks of his, and kiss him there between them. Mmm. I take my time, the way he takes his time, and I can tell as he grows more aroused from the way he shifts against the sheets.

He likes this. My baby likes this.

I oil him up, so gently, so sweetly, my fingers going deep inside of him, and while my fingers work slowly into his asshole, I press my face against his smooth skin and breathe in deep. Oh, is he sweet. He is my angel. My lover. My sweet young thing in a floral dress and tie-up espadrilles, so ready and willing to get fucked against some back-alley wall.

I sit up on my haunches, and I get ready to plunge. My baseball cap comes off, but my hair stays in place, and I'm still him as I work the first part of my thick, ready cock into his asshole.

And as I fuck him, I realize that we've blurred, because there

I am in the mirror. There I am. But who am I? And there he is, his expression one of awe and surrender. And who is he? And more important than either of those questions is this one: Does it matter?

No. Not at all.

Not tonight.

ROOM 2201

N. T. Morley

"Do you remember what I told you last time?" she asked him, the maraschino cherry poised at the edge of her lower lip, neither one appreciably redder than the other. "Do you remember what I told you I would do if you saw me again?"

He didn't answer with words; he just nodded slightly, his eyes lingering over the cherry as she touched it with the tip of her tongue.

She smiled, slipped the cherry between her lips, and plucked it from the stem, chewing it slowly as he watched.

"Do you think I'm as good as my word?" she smiled, reaching across the table to draw the tip of one thumb slowly over his wrist.

His skin goose-bumped at her touch. He shivered slightly. "You've always been true to your word so far," he said.

Her eyes sparkled; she could feel her body reacting. She could feel her nipples hardening under the low-cut white dress. The hint of embarrassment—a residual habit from her earlier life—made her angry, and she growled, holding Marshall's eyes as he looked into her face. He paled, and Caroline sneered.

Every once in a while, she forgot for an instant who she was, and what she was doing. When, moments later, she remembered, she often scared people.

"Then you must want it," she said, lowering her voice slightly as the waiter crept near. "You must want to get fucked."

Marshall gulped, slipped one finger under his tie, tugged at his collar.

"Not really, Mistress," he said, his voice quavering. "I just ... I just wanted to see you again."

Caroline seized another cherry from the mangled dessert she'd barely touched. She put it between her lips. Her eyes stayed locked on Marshall's as she bit down on it slowly, bursting the sodden fruit and letting red juice dribble onto her chin.

She smiled, showing her teeth, filmed slightly red. "I'm so flattered. Perhaps you think I'll let you off the hook? Maybe I won't make you go upstairs and get fucked?"

Marshall's eyes were locked on Caroline's, his breath coming quick. Caroline knew him well enough to recognize the signs—a slight quiver in his hands, a nervous look. If she slipped her hand into his lap, she knew she'd find him hard in those $200 slacks. Knowing that made her wet.

"I don't want to, Mistress," he said. "I'm scared of letting it happen."

Caroline rolled her eyes and leaned back in her chair. If they hadn't been tucked into the corner—a $50 tip to the maitre'd —she never would have done it. But, hidden as they were, she couldn't resist. Her shoe was already off; she'd been toying with it as she enjoyed dessert. Her foot found Marshall's crotch under the table, and he froze, his lips going tight.

He was, indeed, hard.

"Why don't you ask me for mercy, then, Marshall?" she asked him. "Why don't you beg me not to take you upstairs so you can get the living shit fucked out of you? Ask if I'll let you enjoy the evening without having your cherry popped?" She could see the effect her words were having on Marshall, and it egged her on. She smiled broadly. "Why don't you beg me not to lead you to the elevator, take you to room 2201, the room I booked and you paid for, for the sole purpose of seeing me? Why don't you ask me not to take you up there and ..."

Here she might have leaned forward and gotten close to him, lowered her voice—would have, a month ago, when she was slightly more green and slightly less clear on just how much this all turned her on—but instead, she pushed her stockinged foot firmly against Marshall's cock and lifted her arms, stretching with a slight pelvic thrust that was impossible to miss even though Marshall couldn't, strictly speaking, actually see her pelvis.

"... fuck your ass?" she said, just loud enough so that if there had been a waiter or waitress or busboy or hostess coming around the partition at that very moment, that person would have heard it, clearly, with little possibility that he'd misheard Caroline.

Marshall whimpered slightly.

"I want to go upstairs, Mistress," he said. "But I don't ... I don't want to get fucked."

Now she leaned forward, suddenly removing her foot from Marshall's crotch, relishing the dramatic gesture despite the fact that the quick shift of her body put a hint of pressure on her upper thighs, making her head swim.

"Then ask," she snapped, covering her sudden and intense arousal with a snarl.

It took Marshall a long, tortured minute, or perhaps two, to find the words.

"Please, Mistress," he said softly. "Please don't fuck me."

Caroline smiled, as if considering it.

"You haven't made me another offer," she said.

"I ... I could use my mouth," he said. "If you'd let me."

Caroline's eyes found the corner of the room. She displayed a studied look of boredom.

"You could ... hurt me."

Caroline's eyes snapped to Marshall's, and her smile returned.

"Hurt you," she said. thoughtful. "Yes, yes. I like that. Anything else?"

Marshall looked at her blankly.

"Money?" he said, finally, with a meek crackle to his voice.

"Don't insult me," she said.

"Sorry, Mistress, sorry. You could ... you could hurt me a lot. I can take a lot of pain. Remember?"

She sighed, leaning back and returning her foot to Marshall's crotch. "Don't," she growled softly, "insult me."

"Sorry, Mistress," said Marshall, his cock stirring against her foot as he squirmed. He remembered vividly, as she did, that she could hurt him just as much as she wanted, and last time she had wanted a lot. "Anything," he said. "Anything at all." His voice became a whisper—hoarse and terrified. "Just please don't fuck me."

"Well," said Caroline. "I might let you off the hook," she said. "Except ... he's already upstairs."

It took a moment for the words to sink in. His eyes narrowed, went wide, narrowed, went wide again. Caroline could almost hear the gears grinding in his brain.

Caroline sighed and stretched again, as if bored, as if lazy. "He's been waiting up there, watching all sorts of pay-per-view porn—it's on your tab, after all. I'm sure by now he's plenty horny and ..."

She smiled.

"I would just feel so bad telling him he couldn't have your virgin ass, after all," she said.

She removed her foot from Marshall's crotch and stood. The maitre'd, fortuitously between seatings, saw her from across the room and quickly retrieved her shawl.

"Meet you at the elevators," she said, bending down and kissing Marshall on the cheek.

She could feel him shivering.

The maitre'd draped her shawl over her shoulders, and Caroline left the restaurant.

When she glanced back, Marshall was looking through his wallet for his credit card with quivering hands.

The restaurant was in one corner of the Beaumont Hotel lobby; Caroline took her time sauntering across the expanse. He caught up with her at the express elevator, trying not to look as if he was running across the lobby, but succeeding only in sending the message that he was late, terribly late, and eager to get where he was going.

There was no reason to rush. She'd said she'd meet him by the elevators. There was no reason for Marshall to rush after her. No reason at all.

A little surge went through Caroline under the long silk dress.

She was in her twenties, slim, caramel-colored, of mixed Asian parentage with coal-black hair and a group of tattoos up and down her arms, legs and back. When she started out, she couldn't afford fetishwear or equipment; she'd seen guys dressed like the college student she was, in jeans and a wife-beater, in cotton underwear when she bothered to wear any.

Nowadays, while she could have afforded the best gear in the world—or, rather, Marshall could, among others—she didn't bother with all that, because the thought of having to figure out all those whips and chains and straps and zippers made her eyes cross with boredom.

To make up for her lack of gear, she'd gotten good with the mindfuck, and she liked two things about that single and awesome implement of punishment and arousal: First, it made her pussy so goddamn wet she could scream, and second, it was free. Or at least really, really cheap, since Armand had insisted that she pay his bus fare to the Beaumont. He had a bus pass, but Caroline got the sense that he enjoyed feeling like a whore.

He had left his combat boots, leather jacket, and half-shredded jeans in a messy pile near the door. He sprawled on the bed, his muscled body naked except for underwear and a wife-beater, his tattoos evident from shoulder (a Vargas girl locked in unholy congress with a Tom of Finland stud) to waist (the butt end of a Luger sticking out of his jockeys) to calves (twin cobras tangled in his dark hair). His cock was already hard, presumably from the crappy made-for-cable soft core that was playing on pay-per-view. Armand was such a cheap date.

Marshall stood there behind Caroline. She could hear his breath coming short, and knew his eyes were roving over Armand's body—as taut and terrifying an implement as any paddle, whip, or dildo he'd ever experienced in the past. Caroline could feel the heat coursing through her body as she smelled Armand's body mingled with the clean aroma of the hotel room, and fantasized that she could scense Marshall's fear as he cowered behind her.

"Armand, this is Marshall," said Caroline breathlessly, her voice husky from her intense arousal. "Marshall, Armand."

Nervously, Marshall came around from behind Caroline and

extended his hand for a handshake.

Armand looked at Marshall's hand as if it were a dead fish.

He snarled something in Italian. Marshall recoiled as if burned. He looked at Caroline desperately.

"Armand doesn't speak English," she explained. "But I think the two of you can speak the language of love." Caroline beamed.

"What did he say?"

She could barely get the words out, she was so fucking hot.

"He said, 'Tell the faggot to get his clothes off and suck my dick.'"

Marshall caught his breath.

"I didn't know you spoke Italian," he said.

"Only the dirty words," said Caroline.

Marshall stared at Armand, spread out there on the bed, looking angry. Armand pulled down the waistband of his jockeys and his cock popped out, enormous and dark. He looked at it, and then at Marshall, impatiently.

Marshall gulped.

"Should I ..." he asked, unable to tear his eyes away even to glance at Caroline.

Caroline sighed, rapturously.

"What do *you* think?"

His hands shaking worse than ever, Marshall started to undress.

In fact, Caroline's translation was only the roughest approximation of what Armand had said. Not even that, really. On a few key points the two sentences differed entirely, but the point had been made. It had been a bit of a gamble that Marshall didn't speak Italian, but then, Caroline was known for gambles.

Armand watched impatiently as Marshall took off his suit coat, tie, dress shirt, shoes, socks, and slacks, in that order. He stood there nervously in his $50 boxers.

"All of it," said Caroline, who had not taken off a stitch.

Armand reached over to the remote and turned off the porn, which had been there, truth be told, at least partially to make sure that Marshall would get it up if he proved skittish about climbing into bed with Armand.

That, Caroline saw as Marshall dropped his boxers, was not going to be an issue. His cock was hard. He crawled onto the enormous bed, looking nervous, unsure of what to do. He seemed to be recoiling from his proximity with Armand, as if the moment their flesh touched it would be over—he would be gay.

"*Desidera un bacio in primo luogo?*" growled Armand.

Armand seized Marshall's hair and pulled him in, their lips pressing together. To Caroline's relief, Marshall's lips parted at the last moment, and she could see him visibly relaxing as Armand took the older man forcefully in his arms and thrust his tongue into Marshall's mouth.

"He says, 'Does he want a kiss first?'" said Caroline softly, but Armand's meaning had already become clear, and she said it mostly to hear herself say it. The second their lips parted, Armand flipped Marshall over on the bed with the skill of an ex-wrestler, which he was, and shoved Marshall down toward his crotch.

"Oh, fuck," Caroline couldn't stop herself from whispering, as Marshall's mouth opened hungrily and he took Armand's cock into his mouth. In a sense it was a crack in her façade, hinting at just how fucking horny this was making her, allowing Marshall an easy out—he was doing this to please her, not just doing it. In its own way, however, her murmured "Oh, fuck" opened her up to it, and she didn't care any more if Marshall knew how horny she was. She reached up behind her neck and pulled the tie that fastened her dress.

Although the dress was ankle-length, there wasn't much to it—bare back, slit up the side, sleeveless—and it took only a small shimmy from Caroline for it to pool around her feet like moonlight. Marshall's eyes flickered up from what he was doing and, Armand's dick still deep in his mouth, he drank in the sight of Caroline, mostly naked. She stepped out of her dress, deciding to leave on the stay-up stockings and high-heeled shoes. She was deeply in love with the way she looked in the former, especially when her legs were spread, and the latter would be useful if Marshall balked at his upcoming defloration.

Marshall's mouth came off Armand's cock; he watched, his eyes rich with love, as the slim Caroline manfully shoved an armchair right over to the edge of the bed, so she could shimmy into it, spread her legs over the arms, and prop her stiletto heels on the edge of the bed. The stockings and shoes were all she was wearing—in keeping with her dating habits, Caroline had gone through dinner, wet, without the benefit of underwear and, nipples hard, without the benefit of a bra. The wandering of Marshall's attention brought a soft slap across his face from Armand, and Caroline was so intensely aroused to see that that she forgot to listen to what Armand said. So she improvised, as her long-nailed hand came down to start rubbing her clit.

"He says to keep sucking his dick," said Caroline, getting the words out with difficulty because her throat felt tight. " 'You're getting fucked by me,' he says, 'not fucking her.' "

Marshall moaned softly as Armand gave him another slap—not hard, just enough to get his attention, to drive home the point: that Marshall was there to suck cock. That made Caroline swoon so fucking hard that she couldn't even be bothered to translate what Armand said, so again she just made it up.

"He's telling me you'd better have as tight an asshole as I promised him," she said, whimpering as she rubbed herself. "He wants to hear you scream when he fucking ravishes you, you little fucking whore bitch."

As Marshall obediently returned to sucking Armand's cock, Caroline rubbed her clit faster, moaning uncontrollably. She watched his lips gliding up and down Armand's shaft, and the effect it had on her was actually frightening. She wanted to scream, she wanted to come, she wanted to see Armand fuck Marshall so hard it hurt.

Her free hand went up to her breast and lazily caressed her own nipple, and for an instant she suddenly got pissed at herself for letting her nails grow, because she wanted, badly, to be able to put her fingers inside herself right then. She did, a little, and quickly decided that she and the manicurist would have to spend some quality time together before she could do that again. She went back to rubbing her clit and she whimpered, moaned, and squirmed in the chair as she watched her man suck the Italian's cock more eagerly.

What had started out, at least nominally, as a tentative blow job had quickly become something that Marshall did with gusto. Armand's head lolled back and he grunted, growled, grunted, and moaned, his hands resting on Marshall's head for a while— which only made Caroline hornier, because she could imagine for a fleeting second that Marshall really was being forced—and then coming up to swiftly strip off his wife-beater. Armand's muscled body glistened in the half darkness as she caught a whiff of his body, the scent masculine, erotic, familiar. Armand looked over at her and winked.

"He says to fucking suck his fucking cock," snapped Caroline as she rubbed faster, her hand moving in a blur. She was close. "He says to fucking polish his goddamned knob and then he's going to flip you over and fuck your ass. He wants to know if you fucking want your fucking ass to be fucking opened up by his fucking big hard fucking cock, but, no, he doesn't fucking care if you want it, he wants you not to want it, you fucking understand, Marshall? He's about to fucking violate you. He's about to violate your fucking asshole. You want to be fucked, Marshall? Huh? You want to be fucking *fucked?*"

Armand's eyebrows made that "Huh?" motion that Caroline found so fetching—in fact, he hadn't said a word. It looked as if he was maybe considering saying some stuff really fast, but pretty much his whole Italian vocabulary had been used up already, so he just looked at Caroline and blew her a kiss.

Caroline stopped, her hand leaving her clit with obvious difficulty. She was so close that she was about to come, and if she did, she'd never have the guts to go through with it.

Her eyes met Armand's, hard.

"Fuck him," she growled. "Fuck his fucking ass."

Armand's cock came out of Marshall's mouth, glistening with spit. Marshall breathed hard as Armand slapped him in the face with it, just like in the porn movies, and Marshall whimpered softly. Then Armand grabbed Marshall's wrist with one hand and his hair with the other, and guided him face-down onto the bed as Armand swiftly mounted him, kneeing his legs apart.

"*La matita non è tagliente,*" growled Armand.

"He says get up on your fucking knees," Caroline said. "He's going to fuck you."

Marshall moaned softly as he rose, his ass high in the air, his cock hard underneath him, bouncing with every movement of his body. Armand had tucked a condom under the pillow, along with a small packet of lube, but once he had the package ripped open and the condom in his hand, Caroline crawled onto the bed and took it away from him.

"Let me," she said, kissing him.

She rolled the condom expertly over Armand's cock and

cracked the lube with a one-handed twist. She drizzled half the lube between Marshall's cheeks, then slipped her thumb into him, listening to the whimper as he was penetrated. The second half of the lube Caroline emptied over Armand's latex-sheathed cock, kissing him deeply as she stroked it.

Then she guided the head up against Marshall's asshole, looking deep into Armand's eyes as she did it.

His eyes did not change, but she could feel the gentle push, then a firmer one, as Armand's cock pushed against Marshall's virgin asshole.

"Push back onto him," growled Caroline as she drew the cockhead around in small circles. "Fuck yourself onto his cock."

It took a moment for Marshall to comply, but Caroline didn't rush him—she was occupied with kissing Armand deeply, and when she heard the gasp from Marshall and felt him settling, first with difficulty and then with comfort, onto Armand's hard cock, she felt a rush that made her want to come so bad it hurt.

With some of her own difficulty, she returned to her place on the armchair, no longer rubbing herself because she couldn't afford to come just yet. She left the bed because she knew Marshall was in good hands, and she also knew that to fuck the way Armand liked to fuck—and the way Marshall needed to get fucked, deserved to get fucked—a girl on the bed would just be a distraction.

It started with long, smooth strokes, twenty, thirty of them as Marshall slowly relaxed, taking the thrusts more easily. Then Armand leaned forward and produced another lube packet from under the pillow, one with thicker lube. He pulled his cock out of Marshall and lubed it, adding the remaining gel to Marshall's now opened asshole. When Armand entered him again, it was clear that playtime was over.

With his larger bulk and impressive muscles, Armand shoved Marshall onto the bed, hard, splaying him out and grabbing his hair to hold onto.

Then he began to fuck Marshall in quick thrusts, hitting so hard that a mewling cry erupted from the older man's body. Soon the pounding was in full force, and both bodies were moist with sweat, the hotel room sharp with the odor of violent sex.

"Fuck, fuck, fuck, fuck," Caroline heard herself whispering as Armand pounded Marshall, and finally she couldn't hold it back anymore. Her hand was between her legs, she was jilling, and she came in a white-hot wave so intense the whole room went dim.

When her eyes uncrossed and the spasms in her thighs twitched down to a dull roar, she saw Armand lifting Marshall onto his hands and knees again, shouting "Venuto! Venuto!" with copious savagery.

"He says come," rasped Caroline, and she realized she must have been shouting. "Jerk your cock and come."

Five strokes, maybe six—that's all it took for Marshall to spurt onto the bed, the scent of his come just reaching Caroline's nostrils as Armand threw back his head and moaned, thrusting deep inside Marshall's ass. Marshall whimpered, stroking his cock even after it had gotten soft, until Armand seized the base of the condom and pulled out, removing it and tying it into a knot. He missed the garbage can by a foot or so, but Caroline supposed he could be forgiven for not quite being on his game.

Marshall slumped forward onto the bed, shivering all over as he continued to stroke his cock, moaning softly.

Caroline got out of the chair and kissed Armand once on the lips. She reached down and patted Marshall's ass, sticky with lube as it was.

She whispered into Armand's ear.

"*'Ringraziamenti per essere la mia femmina,'*" said Armand with enthusiasm.

"He says, 'Thanks for being my bitch,' " said Caroline.

Caroline took Armand's hand and led him toward the shower.

Later, in the taxi creeping down Sixth Avenue, Armand had his hand tucked indecorously between Caroline's legs. Between a pair of deep kisses, he asked her, "Why couldn't I speak English? Was that his idea?"

"God no," she said. "Marshall isn't that creative. He just gave me the basics and I filled everything in."

"Well, thank God he didn't speak Italian. I barely remember any of it. Half the time I was making shit up."

Caroline shrugged.

"I don't think he noticed. He was distracted by the size of your cock."

"No kidding," he said with evident pride.

"Makes two of us," smirked Caroline.

"You free for lunch?" he asked.

Her hand migrated to his crotch and gently massaged his stiffening cock.

"Let's get take-out," she said.

Caroline smiled as she kneaded.

WORKING LATE

Andrea Dale

Jack had to work late again—on a Friday, no less.

Rain sluiced down the windows, the drops and streams sparkling in the gleam of passing headlights. A dreary night. I slipped my wireless headphone over my ear and dialed my husband's number. As I waited for him to pick up, I clicked the icon on my computer to link with his webcam.

I saw Jack's face and heard his voice at the same time. His dark brown hair was mussed; he'd probably been running his fingers through it in frustration. He needed a haircut, too, poor thing.

"Hello, darling," I said. "How's it going?"

"Just finishing up," he said, closing a folder on his desk.

I glanced at my watch. "Good. Just in time."

The tone of my voice had changed with those last words, clear to him even over the phone. He sat taller in his chair, and his gray eyes briefly unfocused. "Yes, ma'am," he said.

I don't think he'd realized how late it was until I mentioned it. He easily gets lost in his work.

"Close your office door."

He briefly left my field of vision. When he sat back down, I asked, "Is anyone else still at work?"

"I don't think so."

His office had a window to the corridor, but the way his desk was situated, he was mostly blocked from outside view by his 30-inch flat panel Apple Cinema Display monitor. Still, better to be safe than sorry.

I reached for my glass of Scotch and sipped. Ice tinkled in the tumbler as I set it back down.

"Get the package I put in your briefcase this morning," I instructed. "Make sure you bring it back in front of the camera."

Well-trained, he didn't open the black velvet drawstring bag, just sat back down and waited.

Jack enjoyed our games just as much as I did.

"Remove the items."

His chest heaved when he saw what I'd packed for him. What I had planned for him.

"Tell me what you've found."

He tried to speak, failed, cleared his throat, and started again. "A pair of small clamps—nipple clamps. A butt plug, and a packet of lube. Ma'am."

"Tell me what you're going to do with them."

Sometimes I gave orders, but often Jack was smart enough to know what I wanted. I mean, duh, they weren't unusual toys. Besides, having him describe what was going to happen heightened the anticipation—for both of us.

My breasts felt heavy, swollen beneath my silk blouse. I didn't need to look to know my own nipples were clear against the soft fabric.

"I'm going to go to the men's room and put the clamps on my nipples. I'll probably have to massage my nipples a little to get them ready for the clamps." Jack looked down at the items on his desk. "I'll coat the plug with lube, and also my fingers, and open myself up before inserting the plug."

"Will you like that?"

It wasn't an easy question and didn't have an easy answer. He had a love–hate relationship with the plug, craved the sensation while aware of how it looked, what it meant.

"Yes, ma'am," he said.

"Then what?"

"I'll come back to my desk, and when you see me, you'll call me with further instructions."

"Good boy. Go on, then."

He vanished from the screen. I leaned back in my leather chair, propped one stocking-clad foot on a half-open file drawer. I knew he wouldn't dawdle. And he knew he'd be in trouble if he didn't get back to his desk in a certain amount of time.

Beneath my skirt, my stretch lace panties were damp. I ran my fingertips lightly over the crotch, smelling my pungent musk. I indulged in a little over-the-fabric petting, enjoying the tease as I imagined what Jack was doing.

The nipple clamps were light ones, just enough to give a little pinch and keep him aware of his chest. They were small enough that they wouldn't be obvious beneath his crisp, eggplant-hued shirt.

He'd stand in the stall with one foot on the toilet, one hand braced against the wall as he gently stretched his own ass with one, then two fingers. The sheen of a light sweat would break out on his brow when he angled the plug and rocked it in and out, readying himself further. When it popped in, his eyes would close. A moment of adjustment, his body rigid, and then he'd sigh ever so slightly.

After that, there was the matter of stuffing his hardening cock back into his pants. I felt a bit of sympathy for him there. We women just didn't have to contend with that problem.

The plug would feel heavy inside him and the clamps would cause a faint throb in his sensitive nubs as he walked back to his office.

I sat upright, putting both feet on the floor when he came back into view. He sat down gently, settling himself into the chair as if he didn't really want to come into contact with the seat.

I was tempted to tell him to drop trou and prove he'd inserted the plug, but, given the risk of his being caught, I didn't. Besides, I *did* trust him.

It just would've been fun to see his face when I suggested it.

"How're you feeling?" I asked cheerfully when he answered the phone.

"Stuffed full, ma'am," he answered. "Thank you."

I couldn't keep the smile off my face. "Are you turned on, Jack?" I asked, my voice low. "Is that plug knocking against your prostate? Do you like feeling full? Is your cock hard?"

The questions were making me hot, that was for sure. My nipples throbbed in time with my clit. Turning him on turned *me* on—the power I felt, knowing my words enflamed him even more than the clips and the plug. That my words were enough to make him do these things.

"Yes, ma'am," he answered.

"Do you still have some lube left?"

"Yes, ma'am."

See? Smart boy, my Jack. Another man might have used it all up getting that butt plug properly situated. But Jack knew how to plan ahead. Some women might go for the dumb type, but not me. I respected intelligence, creativity. It turned me on.

I praised him accordingly.

"Now, Jack," I said, "I want you to open your pants and pull out your cock."

The way the webcam was pointed, I couldn't see his crotch, but I could tell from his upper-body motions what he was doing. Could tell by the look of relief on his face when his cock was free and in his hand.

"Are you fully hard?"

"Not yet, ma'am. Close."

"Use the lube, and bring yourself to full erection."

Oh, Jack's cock. My mouth watered at the thought of it. I'm not the type to think it's demeaning to go down on a man; I love the taste and feel of a velvet-and-steel rod in my mouth. Once, at lunchtime, I'd surprised him at work and hidden under his desk, licking and sucking him and keeping him on the edge for the full hour while he struggled to eat his Thai takeout and catch up on email.

Hmm. I really was overdue to have him come to my workplace and hide under my desk and lick me until I came a few times. After hours, of course, so no one would see his face glistening with my wetness. Then I'd send him off to a convenience store we never frequented to pick something up for me, my juices dried on his face but his skin smelling obviously of female musk.

"I'm fully hard, ma'am."

"Good. Keep stroking yourself, but not enough to come yet."

I imagined his hand gripping his hard, slick length under the desk, sliding from balls to tip, with a little twist at the end to give the head extra stimulation. It was something I loved to watch, but I could imagine well enough.

My toes curled in my stockings. I wanted him. Soon.

"Ma'am!"

"Yes, Jack?"

He was frozen in place, eyes wide.

"I just saw my boss walk by. I ... I need to stop."

Felicity Jordan, his new CEO. He'd admitted he was quite attracted to her. She was a sexy thing, to be sure: forty-five and mature, with a gym-strong body and wheat-colored hair cut in a thick bob.

"No," I said. "Keep going."

He broke protocol then, but I wouldn't hold it against him because he had a valid point. "We agreed this would never interfere with or jeopardize my job."

"And it won't, Jack. Keep going." I smiled again, a fresh wave of desire shivering through me as the game advanced. "I've made arrangements with Felicity. That would be 'Ms. Jordan' to you tonight."

Confusion passed over his face, but to his credit, I could tell his arm was still moving, his fist still stroking.

"She's made sure there's no one else there," I went on. "She also knows your safeword, and we've discussed your kinks. She's going to give you a spanking. When I get there, we'll both help you finish what we've started.

"Get up now and open your office door and let her in."

Jack stared at the webcam. Then, finally, he said, "Yes, ma'am," and disappeared from my view again.

I took another swallow of very fine Scotch. What I didn't tell him was that there was no need for me to drive there. I'd been watching the spanking from Felicity's own office, through her own webcam.

In a little while, I'd just make my way down the hall and join them.

OTTOMAN EMPRESS

Noelle Keely

I became an empress, the first time, by getting out of work earlier than usual. Jeremy usually beats me home by a couple of hours—he works in the suburb where we live, and I have the commute from hell—and spends some of that time doing yoga. But the air-conditioning in our office had conked out on a scorching, humid day, and finally management had taken pity on us, so for once I was home in time to see the full yoga session. (He does it early in the morning on weekends, early enough that if I see it, it's through a precoffee haze.)

Jeremy was so focused that he didn't even hear me come in. He looked up after a few minutes, smiled and said, "Hi, Karla! You're home early!", then went on with his routine.

I quietly watched him as he twisted into apparently impossible poses and held them for apparently impossible amounts of time. And if yoga doesn't sound like a spectator sport to you, you've never seen it done by a handsome naked man you love. It's ... something special.

At the end, he curled into the child pose—kneeling, bent forward so that his body rested on his thighs, arms stretched in front of him.

A great stretch, I'm sure, but to a viewer, at least one of kinky inclinations who's been gawking at naked, bendy man-flesh and is just a bit turned-on, it suggests complete submission, abasing yourself before the empress on her throne. And it opened his buttcheeks slightly, as if he were offering up that vulnerable part of himself.

Seeing him like that made me shudder with want.

We don't play dominant and submissive full-time, or even most of the time. It's a special treat for both of us. Jeremy can go weeks at a time happily and hornily vanilla before he gets the urge to sub, and while I love dabbling in kink, playing domme is hard work.

Despite that, I definitely have my "empress-of-all-I-survey" fantasies.

And seeing him in that position, so humble and yet so elegant, kick-started both my libido and my imagination. I could just picture myself on a throne, Jeremy a conquered and enslaved prince, prostrate before me, waiting to do my bidding.

My nipples perked up, along with my outlook on life.

I flashed to pictures I'd seen of people used as furniture. At the time, they'd struck me more as being aesthetically pleasing rather than actually hot. But wouldn't an empress love to use her captured prince as a household object, to humble him and teach him his new station in life? I couldn't speak for any real-life empress, but my fantasy-self certainly would!

How would Jeremy look with a tablecloth draped over him and some glasses and plates on his back? (Unbreakable ones, of course, but I'd blindfold him and not let him know.)

Maybe balance the candelabra on him? He'd liked hot wax

the times we'd played with it, so that could be entertaining. (On the other hand, we might set something on fire. Like Jeremy—and not in the metaphorical sense. Well, scratch that idea.)

But the pose he was currently in just cried out for one use—and, lucky me, he was right near the couch.

As silently as I could, I sat down and slipped off my shoes, because fetishistic four-inch heels were one thing but the comfy-yet-hideous flat sandals I wore to walk from the train were another.

I put my feet on Jeremy's back, ankles crossed, as if he were an ottoman.

I more than half expected him to squirm away or exclaim "What the hell!" As I said, I can't take for granted that he's always feeling submissive, and he might simply take it as a joke.

I also thought, too late, that it might not be the best idea. He took his yoga seriously, as a spiritual centering as well as a workout, and maybe this would seem inappropriate. For a second, I held my breath, waiting for his reaction.

He seemed to settle deeper into the pose, stretching closer to the floor. I heard a contented sigh, and that soft exhalation darted between my legs and stroked me.

Just to be sure, I asked, "Is this okay, Jeremy?"

"Okay?" he said, his voice low and breathy like it gets when he's feeling subby. "Mistress, it's wonderful."

And that settled it. He never calls me "Mistress" unless he's thoroughly in the zone, wanting and needing to yield, not just play rough. Otherwise, I'm Karla, even if I'm spanking his butt.

I picked up a book from the table by the couch—a science fiction novel that Jeremy was in the middle of—and made myself comfortable.

It was a good story. Under other circumstances I would have been sucked into its interplanetary intrigues and quirky hero.

But mostly I was using the book as a prop, so if he glanced up, he'd see me looking nonchalant, absorbed in reading and apparently not paying any attention to my footstool.

In reality, most of my attention was on him, on the subtle shifts in his position, on the way he was breathing, on how long I'd had my feet on him and how soon I should urge him to get up and move around. I read a bit, but it was hard to look away from the lines of his body, the curve of his butt and spine and neck, the muscles of his legs. Beautiful.

And mine, in a way he didn't usually seem to be. Oh, he was my lover, my partner, my friend—but only rarely *mine* in the primal way that my inner domme, the empress, likes.

The rest of my attention was focused on my own body, which seemed inordinately pleased by my living ottoman. Pleased, as in aching nipples; swollen, slicked labia; a clit that I swear was standing at attention and twitching; a cunt heavy with arousal and need. The longer I sat there, feet on Jeremy's back, the hotter I got.

Finally I decided that he'd been kneeling an awfully long time, even for someone as practiced at yoga as he was—and that I might spontaneously combust soon if we didn't start touching in other ways.

I swung my feet down, then slipped off the couch and onto the floor next to him.

I grabbed a good handful of his hair and raised his head for a quick, claiming kiss. His eyes, before he closed them, looked like he'd been smoking a particularly fine grade of something illegal—glassy and distant, but happy.

"Do you need to get up and move?" I asked, hoping he still had it in him to answer honestly.

"Soon," was the reply, in a small, throaty voice. "A little while longer, though."

Good. I'd been hoping he'd say that.

While I'd been using him as a footstool, I'd kept thinking about his ass, how enticing and exposed it looked.

I kissed him again, then let go of his hair and worked my way down his body. Kissed his spine, ran my tongue over the vertebrae that stood out in relief in his arched back, tasted the clean sweat that glazed his skin. Nibbled at his firm buttocks.

Parted them with my hands and slipped my tongue between, teasingly.

Then not so teasingly, zeroing in on the little ring of his ass, licking at it, pushing my tongue in. Some might say this wasn't terribly dominant of me. So sue me—I enjoy rimming Jeremy, tasting that dark flavor, feeling like I'm breaking all the rules. It makes me wet, knowing I'm doing something that a lot of people (ones who haven't tried it and don't know what they're missing) consider nasty, makes me wet hearing him moan and beg.

Besides, it got him nice and relaxed and slick, so I could slide a finger inside and start fucking him like the delicious slave-prince he, at the moment, was.

Jeremy jumped and made the most extraordinary noise.

I slid my free hand under him and began milking his cock. The anal attention would have gotten him hard anyway, but the way he was reacting, I guessed he'd been erect since I put my feet on his back.

"You make a wonderful footstool," I whispered at him. "I'm going to reward you now. And then you're going to make me come."

Sure, I could have claimed my orgasm—or orgasms—first. Often, when I'm in charge, I do. But at that moment, I wanted to see him shudder, wanted his ass to grip at my fingers, wanted to feel him spurt into my hand.

"Did you like kneeling under my feet? Because I liked having you there. Liked it a lot."

"Yes, Mistress."

"Did you like it enough to come for me now?" I crooked my finger, stroking at his prostate, ran my other hand over his cockhead—and enjoyed Jeremy exploding on my command, my touch.

Afterward, after I made him lick his come off my hand (okay, I helped a little), I took off my clothes and got back on the couch. My captive prince showed his understanding of his new position by licking and suckling and fingering his empress until she screamed and writhed and would have made a mess of the upholstery had the "prince" not known she sometimes squirted when there had been a long, slow build-up.

Only when captive and empress alike had gone away for the moment, and Jeremy and I, both weak-kneed and grinning like fools, started putting dinner together, did I ask him, "I know why that worked for me. Why did it work for you?"

He paused in his salad-making efforts for a few minutes before answering, "It was like sex and meditation together. I was aroused, but completely centered, completely at peace. Sometimes when I'm bottoming, I fight it even though I want it, or I just can't stop thinking long enough to get into the right mental space. But the combination of the yoga pose and your feet on me—that's just so dominant!—it took me there instantly." He set down the knife he'd been using and wrapped his arms around me. "Thank you."

So now, most nights, we snuggle on the couch and watch a movie, or play on our computers, or curl up in comfy chairs and read, like any couple might do, and then go to bed and fuck like sex-crazed, but basically vanilla, weasels.

But sometimes, when Jeremy craves a night of deeper submission, or when I've had the kind of day that grinds me down, makes me feel small, and I need something to counter it, the empress sits on her throne, and puts her feet on her captive prince, her human footstool.

And it is a good night in the ottoman empire.

CITY LIGHTS

Kathleen Bradean

The man behind me in the airplane's aisle bumped against my laptop, almost knocking it from my shoulder. Crowding me wouldn't get him into the terminal any faster. Rows ahead, another man took his sweet time taking his carry-on from the overhead bin while the rest of us waited. Such a petty power trip. I longed to give him a lesson in manners, delivered smartly across his backside, but that much-needed discipline would only have blocked the aisle for everyone else.

Michael took my bags from me when I finally got off the plane. "Bad flight?"

"Hellish. We sat out on the tarmac for two hours with no air conditioning before they cleared us for takeoff. It was stifling. A crying baby. People bickering with the poor flight attendants—as if that ever helps anything. All I want is a shower and a cold drink."

He didn't say anything until we were in the taxi. "You forgot."

"I won't tolerate pouting, Michael."

The driver glanced at us in the rearview mirror. I met his gaze until he looked away. Michael stared out the window, still pouting. I'd have to do something about that when we got home.

Although the sun had already set, the buildings, roads, and sidewalks around us radiated heat. The air-conditioning in the cab couldn't keep up. I shoved tendrils of hair off the nape of my neck and felt a bead of sweat.

"It's just that being invited over to Harold's for dinner is a big, big deal. It would be professional suicide to beg off."

Dinner with his boss. It was on my planner. Somewhere between the long flight and the delays, I'd forgotten it.

"You don't want to go. You're too tired."

I almost admitted he was right. Then I saw that flash of need in his eyes. And worse, I saw hurt. "No. It's okay. You said this was important. You can't afford to skip it, so we'll go. Just don't expect me to be great company."

Having gotten his way, my man was all smiles. It would be so easy to let it slide just once. Yet, the key to discipline was consistency. No matter how exhausted I was, for his sake I had to punish him.

At our apartment, I took a quick shower. The warm water almost lulled me to sleep. Instead, I put on fresh makeup and found something suitable to wear.

Michael was always the last dressed. He was a handsome devil, and he knew it. Vanity was the only selfishness I ignored. As I waited for him I shut my eyes for a moment of rest, and immediately knew that was a mistake. I sank deeper into exhaustion.

The couch cushions jostled as he sat beside me. His hands caressed my face. At first his kiss was just a friendly touch of the lips, but he wanted more. I couldn't summon up any energy for him.

"Maybe we shouldn't go," he said, pulling away, petulant again. "It doesn't matter. You just want to get into bed. Never mind that you weren't here last time either and I had to go alone."

A simple tilt of my chin was enough to cow him into silence. My unblinking gaze became too hard for him to meet. He looked at his shoes.

"Stand up."

I unbuckled his belt. It jerked through the belt loops of his pants until I pulled it free. I nodded to the back of the couch. "Pants down."

He tried not to look at me, tried not to seem eager. I saw the excitement, though. Praise or punishment—the important thing for him was the attention. He pushed his trousers and briefs below his knees. Feet planted on the carpet, he bent over the backside of the couch. His palms went flat against the seat cushions.

He startled when he heard the electric motor of our curtains.

I put a hand on the small of his back as a reminder that I expected him to remain in position. Twenty-seven stories below our home, the city glittered in its nighttime glory.

"I love this view."

He couldn't see it. As always, he buried his face into the cushions. The flat plane of his stomach rested against the top of the couch. His bared bottom was five feet away from the glass.

I leaned against the back of the couch and took in the beauty of the city. In the sky overhead, helicopters and planes dashed along their paths. At street level a million individual lives dodged, collided, and flowed. But there, right there, my man and I were still, quiet, and at peace.

I folded his belt into a strap and laid down forty harsh strikes on him. Tired as I was, the sight of him with his pants around his knees and the deep pink of his bottom sent a tight squeeze of interest between my legs. I bent to run my tongue across the small of his back. Then I raised the belt again and brought it down on the sensitive area just under the cup of his buttocks.

I adored his grunt. It came as the layers of pain from his punishment reached a crescendo and he was hard. He arched his back, hoping to be fucked, but he didn't deserve it.

What Michael needed was the cane. He clutched at the cushions as the first welt rose on his upper thighs.

"I'm sorry."

"Sorry for what, Michael?"

When he couldn't tell me, I laid down a parallel stroke. He yelped.

"Sorry I was an ass."

The next blow was much harder. His buttcheeks quaked as he screamed into the cushions.

"Relax your muscles, Michael."

It took him a while to get his fear under control. He forced the tension out of his clenched bottom. When he was ready, he got his fourth welt.

"Mistress! I'm sorry I'm so selfish. I'm sorry I pouted. Please! I won't do it again."

While he was apologizing, I gave him the final reminder stroke. When his sobs quieted, I patted his sore bottom. "Pull your pants up, Michael."

His eyes were a bit red, and his clothes were mussed. I gently washed his face and gave him light kisses as I assured him that he was forgiven. He sniffled a little as he nodded. He finally seemed satisfied that he was the center of my attention.

Michael's coworkers were smart, interesting people, and the food was probably great, but I was oblivious. My last reserves of energy flickered warnings of a coming shutdown. From my reflection in the mirror in the powder room, it showed. My eyes drooped.

Every time I hit a wall I somehow managed to gather just enough will to keep going for another ten minutes. There was a limit, though. There had to be a limit.

I enjoyed watching Michael wince when we sat down for dinner. We shared a private smile across the table when he squirmed. Harold saw that and smiled for us, maybe thinking we were very much in love. I enjoyed knowing that Michael's bottom throbbed from his punishment, and that he was probably still hard.

Michael was, of course, the center of attention. People willingly gave it to him. He made sure everyone joined the conversation, and while they spoke, he leaned forward as if fascinated. Sometimes I wondered if his flattery worked on me too. If Harold minded that Michael monopolized the conversation, he didn't show it. Michael's charm was infectious.

After a couple of hours of polite chitchat, I knew that I wasn't up to further banter. As soon as I could slip away without interrupting the conversation, I slipped into Harold's home office. The buttery-brown leather couch looked dangerously comfortable. I experimented with several of the switches on the wall until I got subdued amber lighting from the wall sconces.

The office was nice, the reflection of good taste and lots of money. In a corner was the obligatory telescope. Unable to pass up a chance at having a peek, I checked the focus. I didn't see anything interesting, so I moved the scope around. I found three nearly identical parties going on in other penthouses. I didn't see copies of me staring back. Maybe in alternate lives I was already asleep on the couch behind me, or I was gamely sitting at our host's dinner table trying to make interesting small talk, or I was home in bed.

A sweeping scan of the dark office buildings down the street brought me eye to eye with another searcher. I wriggled fingers in a wave to the man with his telescope pointed at me. Guilt spread over his face. He quickly receded into the darkness of his room. The watchers didn't like to be seen.

I searched further distances. With a laugh of exhausted triumph, I found our apartment. The corner of the living room was the only part I could see, though. The spire of a gothic gray stone building blocked the rest of the view. We'd left our kitchen light on. His belt sat coiled on the floor behind the couch.

"There you are." Michael turned on the brighter lights in the office. "Everyone was wondering."

Harold followed him in, highball glass in hand. "He should get you home. You look beat."

A huge yawn escaped from my mouth to confirm Harold's suspicions. I nodded to the telescope. "Anything interesting?"

"You wouldn't believe the things I've seen." Harold chuckled and shook his head.

"Have a look," I told Michael. "Tell me if you see anything." I turned back to Harold. "Lots of wicked people in this big city."

"It's amazing, the types of things people get up to."

Michael looked up from the sight on the scope. He was pale. I pretended to try my luck at the sights, moving the scope and the focus far off our place.

The first thing Michael tried to do when we got home was close the curtains.

I didn't let him. "Prepare yourself for me," I whispered in his ear.

He undressed and got on the bed on his hands and knees. While I changed clothes, he fingered his ass with teasing strokes. His bottom still bore deep pink stripes from the cane.

I leaned against the bedpost while I watched him slide first two, then three, well-lubricated fingers into his hole. He worked plenty of the slick gel inside, knowing that I expected him to be ready for full, hard penetration when I parted his asscheeks.

He knew I'd punish him if he dared cup his balls or stroke himself. Sometimes he did it anyway. I didn't watch because of that. He confessed those sins eagerly. I watched because he was so damn sexy.

"That's enough play. Come out to the living room."

He flinched.

"Michael."

"With the curtain open? People can see."

"Yes."

"Let's stay in here, please."

"Crawl out there now."

"Please. I'll do anything!"

"You'll obey me, Michael, or you'll pack a suitcase and go to a hotel."

I let him think about it for only a moment before I grabbed him by his hair and dragged him out to behind the couch. He shied away from the windows and turned his face away, but I saw how hard his cock was.

The big purple dildo fit snuggly into the harness ring. It sat above my pussy. I slicked it with plenty of lube even though he was prepared. I kneeled behind him and carefully pushed the thick dildo into his hole. As I crooned encouragement he rocked back onto it, taking it deeper.

He moved his hips in circles, looking to find the best angle for penetration. His ball sac bounced as I grabbed his hips and made shallow thrusts. His head hung down. I dug my fingers into his hair and forced his face toward the window. In the glass, I saw his reflection. He was afraid, but he loved it.

I dripped lubricant on my palm and wrapped my hand around

his cock. Sounds of slick thrusts joined the quiet intensity of our deeply drawn breaths. My penetrating strokes were timed with my sliding grip on his shaft.

His mumbled curses gave way to moans. Soon he set the rhythm. His bottom slapped against my pelvis.

I loved to watch that muscled ass get fucked. My fingernails ran down the backs of his thighs. Gently scraping his testicles made his back muscles shimmy.

He arched his back. "Please fuck me. Hard. Please." Each harsh thrust pushed a grunt out of him until the dildo was buried to the hilt inside him. Then I held still. He tried to buck, but a couple of harsh smacks on his bottom warned him to hold still. "Please fuck me," he whimpered.

"Hush." I slipped my fingers inside me. For such a tired girl, I was very wet. My clit was swollen and enjoyed every stroke that I brushed against it with my fingertips.

"I need to be fucked."

"You need to obey."

He endured it, because he knew from my tone that I'd had enough of his need for the night. "May I lick you?" he offered. When he realized he was being selfish, he always tried to make up for it.

I slowly withdrew the strap-on from his hole. Then I rammed back in, pulled all the way out, and back in again. My thumb pressed against the span between his hole and his scrotum. He hummed, the sound he made when he fought back climax. The reflection of his face in the window showed his deep concentration.

I worked my hand over the head of his cock. Forming small circles with my fingers, I slid over his glans and stroked his full length. He turned to face the floor and huffed every time the swollen head of his cock pushed through that tight ring. I jerked

on his hair. "Let them see how you like being fucked, Michael."
I forced him to face the city.

His balls contracted. I saw his sphincter tighten around the
strap-on. He cried out once and spurted into my hand. I held the
week's load of come on my palm in front of his face. He licked
it off.

He crawled behind me into the bedroom. He bumped his
head against my thighs, nuzzling his way between my legs. I
braced one foot on the nightstand and spread my outer lips for
him. He lapped at me like a man denied water too long.

The air of the room was heavy with the scent of him. His discarded suit was draped across the foot of the bed. My suitcases
sat unpacked near the bathroom door. I was becoming a visitor
to my own home.

I pressed against him. His nose tweaked high on my clit, giving me something of substance to ride. I closed my eyes, closed
out everything but him and me, shut out every thought outside
of sensation. His teeth pulled lightly at my clit. My calves trem-
bled. I touched his shoulder for stability. He stiffened his tongue
and darted it into me. Swooping, pulsing, rushing—orgasmic
waves coursed through my body.

I bent to kiss his face, anointed with my juices.

I should have spent some time planning a harsh regimen for Sat-
urday morning, something that would exhaust him by the end of
the day, something that would sate his endless need, but instead
I rolled over and pressed my cheeks against his chest.

"Do you think anyone saw me?" he whispered.

"Yes," I assured him. "Everyone looked, and while I was
fucking your ass, they wanted to be you."

"Mmm." He nuzzled against me, content.

I didn't admit that his boss had no view of that part of our apartment. The gray stone building between blocked all but the last two feet of the room. There were limits to how far I'd go to humiliate someone, even if he loved every second of it. In a way, it didn't matter. A thousand other people could have seen us. The drapes were wide open, welcoming the watchers. There were so many telescopes out there, and far more dark windows than city lights.

FEEDER

Adelaide Clark

They say that the way to a man's heart is through his stomach, but what the mysterious "they" don't know is that the way to my pussy is also through a man's stomach. Just so we're clear—I get off on watching guys eat. Not just any guys, and not just any food, but my boyfriend, under my direct supervision. You could say it's part of my housewife fetish, but really, it's a lot more than that. Men's lips are the opposite of their cocks—soft and yielding, curving and delicate. When I'm stroking my boyfriend Ron's cock, I always like to stick my finger in my mouth and then trace it over his lips. I make him wait before slipping the finger inside. His mouth always opens for me, lets me enter, take over. It's wet and warm and soft and alive, kind of like my own sex, so maybe that's why I like it.

But anyway, my favorite form of foreplay is to make an extra-special meal and then feed it to Ron in slow, sensual bites. I don't do it all the time, or he'd be thin as a reed, because these snacks aren't so much about his nourishment as his submission. Sometimes I bind his arms behind his back with rope, so all I see before me, under his floppy brow of jet-black hair and those piercing blue eyes, are his open mouth, pink tongue slightly visible, and cock straining against his pants. I'll be stirring something over the stove and he'll come up behind me, nuzzling my neck, his hands going around my waist, most often trying to get beneath my apron. All I have to do is *tsk* once, and he gives me his puppy-dog look of contrition. I wouldn't really say I'm a cook, and am just as happy eating cold cereal or a peanut butter and jelly sandwich, but cooking for Ron brings out a whole other side of me.

He's the kind of guy who frequents five-star restaurants for work, since his job as a publicist requires him to schmooze with editors all day long. I know that sometimes he heads over to Peter Luger's and indulges in a thick, juicy steak with his friends. I'm not always perfect about it, but I try to avoid red meat myself. Still, that hasn't stopped me from jerking off on those nights when he's all suited and tied, hair slicked back just so, or from picturing him cutting into that red, oozing slab of flesh, his hands slicing it into tiny bites like a child, then lifting each one to those precious lips. I picture things I can't see, like the meat once it's placed inside his mouth, getting masticated into tiny pieces. I slip my own fingers into my mouth and suck on them, hard, while plunging my other hand into my panties, as I wish I were there to watch, or supervise, to observe two men doing something men all over the world must do every day—enjoy a meal together, savor what's on their plates in ways that are so troubling for women that we rarely indulge in that ultimate sensual pleasure with quite so much vigor. If it were just Ron and me, alone, I'd make him cut his meat with my bulging breasts right in front of his face, trying to distract him. Then I'd take each almost-raw (his favorite) piece and put it into his mouth myself, feel it slip from my fingers onto his tongue, maybe rub it in for good measure, then let go, letting my meaty fingertips linger under his nose for a moment. I'd watch him swallow, his eyes wide, fixed on me, the pleasure of eating converted into a different type of pleasure entirely as he does it under my gaze.

Watching him deal with the mixture of uncertainty and arousal gets me even wetter. I know that, as much as he loves me, Ron still thinks I'm more than a little weird, but he knows he is, too, because he gets off on my feeding fetish just as much as I do. It doesn't even really matter what I make. It could be a salad, could be stir-fry, could be even humble macaroni and cheese (believe me, I have a cookbook full of recipes for my favorite comfort food, and none of them are humble). Whatever it is, I still get off on mastering those pretty lips of his.

Last night, I decided to try a new recipe I'd found in a magazine. It was a simple recipe, but still a little more complicated than my usual fare—miso-seared salmon with edamame sauce, and a pumpkin and blueberry tart for dessert. I started out by giving Ron my voluminous shopping list, throwing in a few extra items just to add to his subservience—after all, my housewife fantasy only goes so far, and it works as a fantasy only because I don't take it literally. I watched his cute ass head out the door, and began getting out the various pots I needed, whistling as I did so. I made the bed, and even vacuumed the living room rug, doing the few chores that I actually enjoy. When I knew he was about to return, I stripped out of my sundress, leaving my body totally naked, and wedged my feet into my favorite stripper shoes.

I've never been a stripper, and have never worn these shoes out of the house, but they serve their purpose well. They're made of shiny-black patent leather, with a five-inch heel, and are so narrow that I literally have to shove my feet into them. The first time I tried them on, I was sure they wouldn't fit—I've never had narrow feet, by any stretch of the imagination. But, as if a gift from some naughty deity, my feet slid right in, and the shoes felt only slightly pinched, a discomfort that was more than outweighed by the way my red toenails peeked out from the small holes at the tips, the way my feet arched perfectly, the way I suddenly gained enough height to adopt the haughty poise I'd felt accustomed to all my life. Plus, they were just plain slutty, clearly s-e-x disguised in the form of a shoe; I bought them on the spot.

Now, when I want to go the extra mile, I wear the shoes, and only the shoes, as I cook. I heard Ron's key in the door and hobbled over to the kitchen—not to help him, but just to watch him lumber in with bag after bag filled with the ingredients I'd requested—salmon fillets, miso, edamame, tofu, cloves of garlic, vegetable broth, lemons, and butter, flour, sugar, pumpkin filling, blueberries, eggs, and honey for the dessert. Truth be known, we have some sugar in the cabinet, but we can always use more, and the sight of his straining muscles had my pussy clenching already. I grabbed for the miso and took out a bottle of soy sauce and began combining them, handing Ron the recipe so he'd know which items I needed when. I beckoned him over with a curled finger, and practically melted at the sight of his rumpled T-shirt and the eager look on his face. I slipped my finger into the salty mixture and held it out to him, watching as his lips fastened around the outstretched tip, delicately suckling on my offering, his tongue stroking my digit even after that single drop was gone. I pulled my finger out and pointed to the floor, where he dutifully knelt, waiting for his next treat.

I coated the salmon in the miso, then put it in the fridge and began sautéing garlic. When the oil was popping slightly, I made Ron stand over it, knowing that tiny licks of flaming oil would strike his arms, almost infinitesimal drops that he'd barely notice before they disappeared. I let him sauté for just a minute as I prepared the tart ingredients, whisking the flour, sugar, and salt for the pastry dough, one eye on the recipe and one eye on him as my naked body moved about our small kitchen swiftly and efficiently. The faster I cooked, the sooner I could hand feed my gorgeous stud slave. I got the pastry dough ready and rolled it out into the pan. As I reached for the blueberries to wash them, I crushed a few between my fingers, watching the indigo juice sluice down my palm. Ron was kneeling again, his face peacefully blissed-out; I think these cooking sessions are like meditation for him. His T-shirt was one of those simple ones that come in a three-pack, so I took my blueberry-smeared hand and wiped it from his cheek down his neck and across his shirt, leaving him a sticky mess. He whimpered as I towered over him in my heels, and I shoved three fingers into his mouth, knowing he wasn't quite prepared for that. When I want to, I can get my whole fist in there (small hand, big jaw), but I just wanted to tease him. He's a bulky guy, but he looks so much smaller when I'm in my heels. I took pity on him and pulled my fingers out, then leaned forward, pushing my breasts together with my hands and letting him suck on my nipples. His tongue immediately started flicking, and my pussy tightened in response. Part of me wanted to plant my legs on either side of his face and have that be his dinner *and* dessert, but I held off. By the time he was done eating, his fat cock would be more than ready to fuck me into oblivion.

I returned to the stove, getting the tart in the oven, blending the edamame, garlic, and seasonings, and finally it was time to take the salmon out of the fridge. I did, then poured the oil into my skillet, watching it drizzle out like lube. When I had enough, I dropped each fillet into the oil, then added the glaze. Four minutes and they were perfectly sizzled, the air permeated with their delicious scent. I slid them out of the pan and onto one plate, then carried it over to the dinner table after I'd turned the oven off, letting the tart stay until we were ready. I have a special beanbag chair I bought Ron for our first anniversary, which I dragged over from its corner to the space below my seat. I planted my bare ass down in my seat, then covered my lap with a cloth napkin—no need to skimp on propriety just because I was naked and my boyfriend was splattered with blueberry. "Are you hungry, baby?" I asked, as I lifted my first forkful of salmon to my mouth. It tasted divine, perfectly savory, the fish practically sliding down my throat. "Hmmm," I said, cutting another piece for myself. I had both fillets on my plate and could have handily finished them off, but this was about more than the hunger rumbling through my stomach. I patted my lips, then turned my chair slightly and spread my legs so he could see my other lips. I left my napkin on the table, watching his eyes move from my pussy to my face to my plate, trying to figure out which one he wanted the most.

I made the decision for him. "Open wide," I said, and brought my salmon-filled fork to his mouth. His body seemed to melt against the tines as he let me penetrate his lips with my offering. He was dainty and polite, almost girlish, as he delicately took the morsel of food from the fork, sliding it over the metal spikes and into his mouth. I pulled the fork back but left the sharp edges hovering right next to his lips, leaving just the briefest of spaces between his soft, wet, pink lips and the hard stainless steel. He chewed, a rapturous look on his face that I inhaled in my own way, my pussy clenching as I watched those lips move, watched him savor every bite. All the diet books say that when you're eating, you should only be eating, taking the time to fully taste and savor every bite. Well, in our household, we don't need anyone to tell us that. It's our standard MO, and I bet there'd be a lot more thin men in the world if their wives or girlfriends chose to feed them this way once a week. The whole ritual took about a minute, from my hand leaving my plate to his final swallow, his eyes peering back at me, radiating the unique kind of lust between one who knows he's thoroughly beholden to his true love, and one who takes that responsibility quite seriously. Suddenly, I was done with the salmon myself, and pinched off pieces of the warm, pink meat between my fingers and gave them to my boyfriend. Sometimes I left them in the palm of my hand and made him lap them up like a cat. By the time the last bite was gone from my plate and he'd dutifully licked it clean, my chair was almost in need of some dry cleaning—yes, that's how wet feeding Ron makes me.

I didn't even bother with the tart. I was staring down at my dessert as I took the sole of my shoe and pressed it lightly against Ron's crotch, the heel digging into the beanbag. "Adelaide," he moaned, my name coming out deep and husky, shooting right into me. I slipped off the chair and onto the floor, reaching for his zipper. Our lips met and I tasted the tangy remnants of our dinner on his breath, the traces of lemon, the hint of garlic, the flavor of salmon. I shoved my tongue deeper into his mouth, licking his teeth, tangling with his tongue. I was the ravenous one now. While only minutes earlier I'd wanted him to fuck me, now I needed to taste his cock. I yanked down his zipper and pulled out his dick, which looked even bigger than usual, full and hard and warm. I leaned down and took him into my mouth in one smooth stroke. I didn't have time for playing games, for waiting any longer, and I pushed my lips down his shaft until they brushed against the wiry hair poking out from the base. I gagged, in the good way, knowing I'd done my job right.

I moved my body to the side, so that I was perpendicular to him, on my knees, so he could reach my cunt. He knew what to do, and immediately slammed three wide fingers into my aching slit. I gobbled him up, my own private dick-feast, not caring how much saliva dripped down my chin or how I looked, I just wanted as much of him inside me as I could get. This is the other side of my domme act, my inner slutty housewife emerging from beneath the veneer of control. Because with us, it's a two-way street. Neither truly controls the other, unless you count the sheer, overpowering desire we each have for the other's body. I grabbed his blueberry-stained T-shirt in my hand, caressing the soft fabric, bunching it between my fingers as my other hand circled the base of his dick while he pushed and stroked exactly where I needed him. I groaned against his cock, practically gargling, my mouth was so wet, as I challenged myself to take even more of him. I slowly moved up and down along his saliva-soaked dick while he did, indeed, fuck me senseless, plunging his fingers in and out of my hole relentlessly until from both ends I was a dripping, sloppy, greedy mess. I needed his fingers in my cunt as much as I needed his cock in my mouth, and my boyfriend gave me both, our bodies perfectly in sync as I spasmed against his fingers, coming so uncontrollably I had to pull my mouth off his cock. I used my hand to jerk him off against my tongue, letting his dick slap against my lips and tongue until he fed me a treat of my very own—his piping-hot come, erupting all over my mouth as I scrambled to swallow it all.

After, my body was spent, my pussy still trembling just enough that I could feel the tiny shivers along my lips as I lay on the floor, head on my arm, looking over at Ron. We exchanged silent smiles, "feeder" and "feedee" turned feedee and feeder, two hungry mouths and horny bodies and swollen hearts. He lifted the T-shirt over his head, turned it inside out, and nestled it under my head as a pillow. Only much, much later did I slide the cooled-off tart out of the oven, spooning one bite to me, and one to him, over and over, until our appetites were finally sated.

PENELOPE THE PUNISHER

Stan Kent

With Jasmine "Caning" Able in firm control, it didn't take much persuading to convince Penelope to return to Renforth Manor—the renowned school of executive motivation nestled in the quiet English countryside where CEOs in dire need of motivation for their burned-out careers were treated like schoolboys and their teachers were blackmailed into performing as submissives for them as a front for the production of kinky S/M videos. Penelope was eager to exact her revenge for having been duped into serving as a toy for the executives and school administrators. To celebrate her triumphant return as a domme, Ms. Crumleigh dressed in a latex storm trooper's uniform she'd had custom made for regular spanking sessions with a wealthy client who'd been a prisoner of war. With riding crop in hand, her pretty blonde hair tucked inside a shiny, peaked cap, and leather riding boots in need of a tongue polishing, Penny had entered Headmaster Rust's study, exiting bleary-eyed the next morning with her boots glistening to perfection, the crop broken in two.

The headmaster didn't make an appearance for several days.

Her revenge on the vicious head boy, Alexander Trent, who had masterminded her downfall, came next. Jasmine had one of Renforth's old basement cellars outfitted as a dungeon for the punishment. In much the same way that he'd taken advantage of Ms. Crumleigh in her naïve days, Trent was drugged with doctored port. He awoke on a rack, the revenge-minded young teacher pacing at his feet. Penny was dressed and made up to look like Trent's mother, the very prim and proper Lady Trent. Jasmine went to great lengths to find the right well-to-do clothes, including the garden party hat under which Penny's long, golden locks were hidden. Completing the disguise was a sinister black-leather eye mask designed by Jasmine to nightmarishly contrast with Lady Trent's genteel floral hat. Penny's appearance wouldn't have fooled a keen-eyed passport officer, but a drugged and frightened young head boy was easily duped.

The schoolboy executives were an integral component of Penelope's revenge. They lined the dungeon walls, dressed in hooded executioner garb. Flaming torches illuminated the room, to maximum medieval effect. Jasmine stood behind Penelope with Packstowe and Justice on leashes. Dressed as wolfhounds, the prefects were instructed to bark and howl or risk Caning Able's wrath. If they gave the game away to Alexander, they too would face the rack. They howled magnificently.

As the drug wore off, Trent stirred, his head rolling. Jasmine nodded to Penny to begin. Ms. Crumleigh walked over to the head boy and cradled his head, offering him a bowl of water. It was a dog's metal bowl with "Alexander" engraved on it.

"Here, my son, drink. You must be thirsty."

Trent lapped, coughing as water filled his throat.

Penelope pulled the bowl away, making sure that Trent's clearing vision registered his inscribed name.

"You've been a very naughty boy, my son."

"Mummy?"

"Yes, Alexander, it is Mummy, come here to punish you for abusing all those young ladies. You've been a dog, Alexander, a shameful hound, and I'm here to train you, as I would one of my hunting dogs that had behaved badly."

Penny dashed the remaining water in Trent's face and grabbed his wet cheeks, pinching the loose flesh, kissing him full on the mouth.

"There, Alexander—that's so that you know I still love you. No matter what I must do to you, you know that Mummy loves you."

"Mummy loves me?"

"Yes, Mummy loves you. Why else would I allow you to watch me dress? Oh yes, all those years ago I knew you were eyeing my naked body as I slipped into my lingerie. Of course Mummy loves you, but she must also punish you. Now, Alexander, you see all these shadowy figures surrounding us? They are your jury. Do you hear the hounds at your feet?"

Following a swift kick from Jasmine's stiletto boots, Packstowe and Justice did a passable imitation of the Hound of the Baskervilles having his balls squeezed. Trent struggled against his bonds.

"Mummy, Mummy, why are you doing this to me?"

"You were cruel to a young woman teacher, Penelope Crumleigh. Do you remember her?"

Trent's timorous voice slid from him as he regressed further into the role of a disciplined child.

"Yes, Mummy."

Penny screamed into Trent's ear.

"You drugged her, you seduced her, you blackmailed her, you beat her, you made her suffer the lewd advances of your friends, and then you turned her out like so much dog shit on your shoes."

Penny stopped yelling. Lady Trent would never lose control. After a deep breath she resumed her unflappable English-lady pose.

"That's what you did, Alexander, and now you must pay. Take your punishment like a good boy, and prove to these stout fellows that you are truly sorry, and you'll live to see another day. If you fail—do you see the lady behind me? She's a friend of mine, Ms. Whore."

Penelope pointed at the masked Jasmine, who acknowledged Trent's stare by making Justice and Packstowe howl and tug on their leashes. Penelope ended her speech by screaming into Trent's ear.

"If you fail to show you're sorry, Ms. Whore will turn the hounds loose on you to rip the flesh from your worthless bones, starting with your dick."

Trent whimpered his response through choked-back sobs.

"I'm sorry, Mummy. I'm sorry. Please forgive me."

Penelope regained her Lady Trent–like composure.

"It's not enough to say it, Alexander. You have to prove it. Mummy wants you to show her how sorry you are."

"I will, I will. I'll do anything you want me to do to prove how sorry I am for hurting Ms. Crumleigh."

"I'm so happy to hear you say so, Alexander, because by the time I've finished with you, you may think the hounds' jaws are a better fate."

Penny climbed onto the rack and stood above Trent's head.

"Look up, Alexander. Look up Mummy's dress."

Through squinting eyes, the head boy looked up along the shapely legs he believed to be his mother's. He snapped his eyes shut as if, from staring too long, his mother's lingerie-clad body could turn him to stone.

"Open your eyes, boy, and take a good look. Do you like what you see?"

He'd better, thought Jasmine. She'd gone to tremendous lengths to find just the right blend of elegance and smut, working with a custom corset manufacturer to come up with what Penny wore underneath her sensible, orange two-piece suit. On her feet were elegant cream-colored high heels. Enveloping her legs were flesh-tone opaque stockings, fastened at midthigh by six white satin ties that clipped to the corset. Her panties were pink silk. The corset remained mostly in shadow to the ogling Trent. Even so, the absence of crisp detail was stimulus enough to a young man with an active libido. The head boy's cock grew stiff and beckoning. Penelope was pleased.

"I see that my undergarments please you, Alexander. I'm so glad you find Mummy sexy."

"I do, I do."

"Good, I'm glad, because you'll enjoy licking my bottom all the more."

Bending slightly, Penny gripped the hem of her sensible suit and pulled it up her legs, bunching the skirt around her waist.

"Silly me. I may as well take this skirt off so you can see how pretty the rest of Mummy's underwear is. I know you like my knickers, Alexander. I know that you go through my drawers, fondling my silky, satin panties."

Penny's voice grew louder. Her acting skills impressed Jasmine. She played the crazed woman down to a tee, screaming at just the right moment and calming without warning.

"I also know that you dress up in them, masturbating your putrid little cock to orgasm in my designer lingerie."

Jasmine smiled. After Trent's admission during his shaving that he watched his mother dress, she had delved into his confidential profile and confirmed her suspicions of Trent's maternal cross-dressing fetish. The public revelation had devastated the head boy.

"I'm sorry, Mummy, I tried to clean it up, but there was so much of it. I didn't mean to ruin your panties. I'm sorry."

"Don't worry, darling little Alexander. Mummy has lots of men who can buy her rooms full of underwear. But she only has one of you, so do please do as you're told. Show me and your judges that you are truly sorry. I'd hate to have the dogs rip off your cock and fight over it like a tossed bone."

As her voice went from a whisper to a scream, Penny settled her skirt to its normal length and reached behind her, unzipping the garment, allowing its descent to her trim ankles. The skirt landed on Trent's face. Stepping out of the garment, Penny smothered the head boy with the crumpled material. He sniffed at the perfume suffused into the skirt's fibers. Penny wore Lady Trent's favorite scent, *Astor*. Using her heel, Penny hooked the skirt and kicked it to the floor, leaving the head boy with olfactory memories of his mother.

"You like watching Mummy undress for you like a cheap, peep-show stripper, don't you, Alexander? I see it arouses you. Would you like a little bump and grind as I take off my top? Too bad you can't rub off like you do when you watch me strip."

Penny swayed her hips in a fine imitation of a stripper's motion as she undid the suit top, button by button, and slid it down her arms. She held it in her hand and whirled it around her head before launching the garment at Trent's twitching cock.

"Do you like seeing what a slut your Mummy is, Alexander? I do hope so. By watching me, you make me even more of a slut, because I do so like exciting my baby boy. It gets Mummy ever so wet to know that she makes her son's cock hard. Now, I think it's time to take off my panties so you can lick my bottom clean."

Penny bent and slipped the silky pink near-nothings down

her legs, anchoring them to her ankles, spreading her limbs as far as the panties allowed.

"Before you lick my bottom, Alexander, I want you to smell my panties, smell how wet you've made Mummy."

Legs spread, Penny bounced up and down on her high heels so that she was able to slide her wide-stretched panties over Trent's face, positioning the vibrating garment above his nose. As she performed her tiny jumps, the scent of her secretions wafted up his nose. As "Mummy's" panties pounded into his face, Trent watched her buttocks ripple and shake with every jigging of her legs. He was in heaven. His face told the story. If this was punishment, let there be more! But Trent had no idea what was in store for him.

Penelope stopped moving and hooked the panties from her ankles, holding them in her hands. She dropped to her knees and wrapped the sodden garment tight around Trent's cock, knotting the silkiness under his balls in an erection-engorging constriction. Inching backward, she pressed her anus into Trent's mouth.

"Tongue your Mummy's bumhole, Alexander. Lick my ass well. Show Mummy you are sorry by sticking your tongue all the way up her anus while I whip your cock as punishment for being such a bad boy."

Trent eagerly complied, slithering saliva around Penny's sphincter with his tongue. Jasmine tossed a studded cat-o'-nine-tails to Penny's outstretched hand. Thanks to the shield of Penny's buttocks, Trent did not see what was about to be unleashed on his unsuspecting penis. Penny felt Trent's rolled-up tongue snake inside her bottom. She pressed her round buttocks into his face, burying his nose into her asscrack. Then she reared up on her knees and brought the cat down hard on the head boy's genitals. He was ill prepared for the shock of the blow. His body convulsed and he screamed into Penny's distended sphincter, but she didn't relent.

"Don't stop, little boy. Mummy's not sure you're truly sorry yet."

As she arched her back, Penny's spasming bottom rudely expelled Trent's scream back into his face. The head boy coughed, his gagging muffled by the snug fit of Penelope's bottom on his face.

"That'll teach you to scream, Alexander. Take your punishment like a man."

With another flash of Penny's arm, the cat lashed out its claws again. Thin red trails snaked across Trent's shuddering loins. To his credit, he didn't scream, but instead he burrowed his tongue into Penny's bottom. He used his tongue like a penis, sliding it in and out, rotating the curled organ inside her anal passage, traversing all the small undulations and bumps. His body was as rigid as a plank, awaiting the next blow. Penny timed it to perfection, snapping the nine tails just as his tongue withdrew from her puckered opening.

Trent head slammed back against the rack. He repeated the motion as if he were trying to stun himself to prevent further pain. Penny allowed Trent no such evasive action. She pressed his head tight against the wooden device with her buttocks. Twisting her neck to look at his muffled face, Penny reassured Trent before transitioning into a vengeful martinet.

"Now, now, Alexander, please behave. Only I can harm you. You must not try to do so yourself. It is a sin, and I'm afraid you do not impress the audience by being such a pathetic, sniveling, wimpy little shit. If I have my way, your cock will first be punished and then fed to the dogs."

Penny leaned forward, placing the cat on the floor, taking Trent's raw cock in her hands. He quaked with every minute touch, the nine studded tails having scored his most-tender skin. Instead of sticking his tongue into her bottom, Trent lapped at her sphincter, making long motions with his tongue along her bum crack. As he did so he whimpered. Still Penny was unforgiving.

"*Alexander*, you try my patience. How dare you lick me like a common animal? I tire of you."

Penny stood and faced the head boy. Her eyes locked on his. She moved along his torso until she hovered above his wounded cock. She looked down at the throbbing instrument, constricted by her pink panties that were now blood-striped from the head boy's wounds. She squatted, taking his battered cock in her hands.

"No, Mummy, please. It hurts so!"

"Ssssh, little boy. Perhaps now you will not abuse women."

"No—no—"

She inserted Trent's torn cock inside her bottom and rode his flailed pole. Each pumping stroke of his tender skin tortured the head boy.

"Mummy, I'm sorry—I'm sorry—I'm sorry—"

The possessed young woman was beyond listening to Trent's pleas, intent on the fullness of his swollen penis in her arse, her hands now focused between her thighs, massaging her clitoris. The head boy had been reduced to a dildo for her pleasure.

"Mummy, I'm coming—I'm coming—I'm coming—"

Trent's body softened as he came, a rude squishing sound emanating from Penelope's bottom as his orgasm was forced through the tight seal of her clutching sphincter. Trent cried. The sting of bodily fluids and rubbing friction on his sore skin was agony, but Penny did not halt her motions. She rode Trent until his softening and battered cock popped free of her anus. Still she did not stop the torture, rubbing herself to a satisfying climax on Trent's now-flaccid cock. With no pause for enjoyment of her release,

Penelope Crumleigh leapt up, glowering at the head boy. The look delivered as much pain as any of the cat's lashes had done.

"You fucked your own mother up the ass, Alexander! You're a vile little shit. If you were truly sorry for hurting those women, you wouldn't have bum-fucked me. You didn't even practice safe sex."

"Mummy, I'm sorry, forgive me. I had no choice. You forced me. Please don't hurt me anymore. I'll be good. I promise."

Penny ignored the head boy, almost falling as she stepped off the table. Jasmine steadied her. Penny teetered back to Trent and bit his earlobe as she whispered to him.

"It's not up to Mummy, Alexander. It's up to these men." She turned and faced the hooded executioners. "Well, gentlemen, is he truly sorry?"

As instructed, all eighteen signaled thumbs down. The head boy looked on in horror.

"No, Mummy, don't let them savage me. I am really sorry. Honest."

Penelope turned to Jasmine and proclaimed, "Cry havoc, and let slip the dogs of Ms. Whore."

Trent's cry of "No!" echoed around the room, refusing to dim. It did no good. Jasmine reached down and unsnapped the leash around Packstowe and Justice's necks. They played out their role to perfection, having been guaranteed no further humiliations if they performed superbly in this scene. After a rabid baying, they leapt on the terrified head boy and pretended to bite and claw at his wounded cock.

Trent's screams were only outdone by Penelope and Jasmine's hysterical laughter as they walked out of the dungeon, arm in arm as the new headmistresses of Renforth Manor.

SHADES OF RED

Lisabet Sarai

"**S**ex with strangers? For money? You've got to be insane, Ruby!"

Jane's delft-blue eyes are wide with disbelief. Her horrified protest is loud enough to trigger tolerant smiles at neighboring tables. This is, after all, worldly and decadent Amsterdam.

"I've already hired the window. For tonight."

"But it's dangerous …"

"Oh, please! There's twenty-four-hour video surveillance. The police practically outnumber the tourists strolling around the district at night. Every cubicle has an alarm in case things get dicey. The landlord showed me how it worked."

"But it's so degrading! Once a man pays you, you're obliged to do whatever he says. You've got no choice."

I sip my cappuccino. My lipstick leaves a crimson crescent on the china cup.

"Nonsense. I'll be the one in control. I was watching the women last night. Anyone whose looks they don't like, they send away. The men are the ones who are desperate, vulnerable. They want us so much, they're willing to pay to satisfy their desires."

Jane shakes her head. "If your father finds out, he'll be furious."

"How would he find out? You wouldn't tell him, would you?" I put on a stern face, not too different from his. Cowed, she lowers her eyes.

"Of course not. Still, you know how he is. It was tough to get him to agree to this trip at all. We had to really lean on the culture aspect."

"I'm old enough to make up my own mind." My friend's red-gold ringlets, backlit by the afternoon sun, make her look like a Botticelli angel. I relish the thought of corrupting her. "Come on, Jane, we've been doing nothing but dreary museums and libraries and concerts for the past three days. I just want some fun."

"I'm afraid you'll get more than you bargain for."

"I certainly hope so. Look, why don't you join me? Last night I noticed quite a few windows with more than one girl. The cubicle has a double bed, and you're so gorgeous, I'm sure you'll be popular."

"Not a chance. Freddie would break up with me in a second."

"What Freddie doesn't know won't hurt him."

Jane looks insulted. "Freddie and I have a relationship based on honesty and trust. I'm not going to do something sordid and risky like that behind his back."

I wonder if Freddie has shared with my poor friend the fact that he has propositioned me, under the pretense of being drunk, at more than one party. Innocence, I decide, is bliss—at least for sweet, loyal Jane.

"Well, why don't you come around with me to the sex shops

anyway, to help pick out a costume and some toys."

"I've got a miserable headache." Jane sounds peevish. I worry briefly that she somehow caught my thoughts about her beau. "I'm going back to the hotel to lie down. Will I see you tonight, before ... I mean, are you going to have dinner, or what?"

"I think I'm too excited to eat. But I've got to take a shower and do my makeup, and that will be easier in our room."

"Okay, see you later. Be careful."

"You know me. The coolest of the cool."

But I'm not. In fact I've been obsessed ever since last night, when Jane and I wandered through the red-light district, staring at the women who waited behind the glass in their rose-tinted rooms. We wove our way through clumps of nervous, intoxicated men who were all staring, too. I could smell their sweat, underneath the beer and the pot smoke. I could feel their lust. It infected me.

They barely noticed us, two teenagers in jeans, although the tight denim in my crotch was so wet, I half-expected they'd catch my scent and turn to me. But they had eyes only for the bodies displayed in the rows of windows lining the canals.

Some of the women were ripe, blond, Slavic-looking, their breasts exploding out of their lace brassieres. Others were slight, deliberately child-like in Gidget-inspired bikinis or brief plaid kilts. There was a Brazilian beauty with golden skin and coffee-colored eyes, a voluptuous African princess with strings of ruby-hued beads dangling in her ebony cleavage, a serious-looking brunette wearing dark-framed glasses who sat, shapely legs crossed, like a secretary waiting to take dictation.

Some of the women posed. Others danced suggestively, or made lewd gestures at their prospective customers. There were masked women in leather, snapping riding crops against their boots. There were women whose pierced nipples and labia showed clearly through their translucent garments.

Men clustered around the dimly lit windows like moths hovering by a candle. Mostly they'd just look, inflamed by the mere thought of all this available flesh. Sometimes I'd see a hushed conversation through a half-open glass door. Such conversations might end with the man turning away, disappointed, rejected, or perhaps simply unwilling to pay the asking price. Other times the door would open wider, just enough to admit the supplicant. Then it would close and the red velvet curtains would be drawn, hiding the rest of the dance.

Those curtained windows drew me. I couldn't stop imagining what might be going on behind them. I knew it was a straight commercial transaction in most cases, a workman-like blow job, or a quick, bored fuck. Still, I imagined occasional revelations, epiphanies, ecstasies—meetings of strangers predestined to be lovers, brief but unbearably intense conflagrations of lust, lewd and mystical connections that would live in his memory, or hers, long after the curtains were flung open again.

I'm nineteen. I've had enjoyable but ultimately frustrating sex with two boys my age. I know that, practical as I am, I'm a bit of a romantic. Otherwise, I would not have continued to roam the red-lit alleys long after Jane gave up and went back to the hotel in disgust. As the Oude Kerk chimed two A.M. I wandered up Molensteeg and down Monnikenstraat like some horny ghost. The crowds had thinned. The curtains were mostly drawn. Some open windows were empty. Next to them were the signs: *Kamers Te Huur*. Windows for rent.

Back in my own bed at the Hotel de l'Europe, I tore off my jeans and sank the fingers of both hands into my aching pussy. I imagined myself lounging in an armchair behind one of the windows, displaying my swollen, soaked sex to the crowd gathered outside. In my fantasy, the men unzipped and pulled out their cocks, stroking themselves in time with my frantic fingering. Just before I came, I remembered Jane sleeping in the other bed. I swallowed my moans as pleasure surged over me in blood-colored waves. The men outside my window came along with me, spattering the window with their semen. The notion sent another climax rolling through me, leaving me limp but still unsatisfied.

I let sleep take me, without showering or even undressing. My dreams were incoherent but lit in shades of red.

In the Chickita Sex Shop, I found the ideal costume: a scarlet leather corset and thong, with fake silver chains looping from the half-cups down through the crotch. I didn't feel embarrassed when I dropped the stainless steel vibrator into my basket, but I admit that the wrist and ankle restraints made me blush a little. The clerk, a buxom forty-year-old in a tight black tee, with magenta hair and multiple tattoos, convinced me to purchase a neat little whip, as well. I really didn't have a clue how to use it, but when she trailed the leather strands over my bare arm, electric arousal whizzed up my spine. "Just follow your instincts," she advised, in excellent English. "I think you'll find that power comes naturally."

Jane watches, torn between horror and admiration, as I lace up the front of the corset, tight enough that my breasts nearly spill out over the top. "I can't believe that you're doing this, Ruby. I just hope you won't regret it."

"I won't. I never regret anything I do." My bravado sounds a bit hollow to my own ears, but Jane's convinced.

"But why?"

"I need to know what it's like. The whole idea turns me on so much—I've just got to try it." The minimalist leather triangle covering my crotch is already slick with my juices. Every time I move, the chains sway against the skin of my inner thighs, making me long for more definite caresses.

I paint my eyebrows into sooty arches, my eyelids purple, and my lips crimson. The effect is a caricature of a Chinese porcelain doll. I fasten my waist-length hair at the top of my head with a silver clasp. It cascades in waves of jet down my back. My own pointy-toed high heels complete the costume. I examine my face in the mirror. My eyes are luminous, my cheeks flushed.

"How do I look, Jane?"

"Glamorous. Wicked. Dangerous."

"Perfect." I throw my coat over the costume and grab the bag with my other paraphernalia, without showing the contents to Jane. I figure she's having enough trouble dealing with the situation. "I'm off. Don't wait up for me."

"Please be careful, Ruby." She looks so young, sitting cross-legged on the bed, her brow knotted with concern.

"I'll be fine. And don't worry—I'll tell you all the details tomorrow."

She groans and shakes her head as I let myself into the corridor.

On the way to the elevator, I pass a waiter delivering room service. "Good evening, Madame." He mostly manages to suppress his reaction to my extreme makeup. I wonder what he'd think if he could see under my coat.

From the hotel to the district is barely a mile. My heels sound crisp and determined on the cobbled pavement. My heart slams against my tightly bound ribs, almost loud enough to drown out the sound of my steps. It's September, and at seven o'clock it's already dark. The narrow merchants' houses loom over black, rippling canals. Rose-colored lights are on in many of the tall windows. Scantily clad women smile and beckon to the thickening crowds. Somehow I can't meet their eyes. I hurry along to my own cubicle on Oudekerksplein, unlock the curtained door, and quickly shut it behind me. I sink into my rented armchair, breathing hard. My nipples are taut and aching, pressed against the leather that constrains them. The chains swinging between my thighs are wet.

The room is dark except for light that filters in from the street along the edges of the curtain. I flip the switch and the space is suffused by a rosy glow. It's tiny, maybe 10 feet deep by 7 feet wide, but somehow it manages to contain a double bed, an upholstered armchair, and a circular three-legged table. A fire hose is coiled high on the wall, with an old-fashioned cast-iron radiator below it. At the front is the curtained glass window/door. At the rear, there's access to an airplane toilet–sized bathroom. Clearly visible, within reach of the bed, is the red alarm button.

The radiator is pumping out heat. I shrug off my coat and hang it on a hook on the bathroom door. My bare skin is damp with sweat. I dump the contents of the sex shop bag on the bed. I'm tempted to turn on the vibrator and slip it into my cunt, but instead I arrange it, and the restraints, on the little table. Last night I noticed some of the women casually displaying dildos or butt plugs or rubber gags. Advertising their specialties.

Of course, I'm hardly a specialist. What if my john is disappointed? I push away my doubts. After all, this is my game. I'm going to be the one in control. My satisfaction is what counts. I'm the one paying for the window.

I'm so nervous that I need to pee. The hot liquid flowing over my swollen tissues feels exquisite. My clit throbs, begging for my attention, but I manage to resist. Soon, I promise myself. Soon I'll have a thick, hard cock between my legs.

I seat myself in the chair, one heel up on the seat so that my juice-smeared thighs are spread. I drape the whip over the other thigh. Then I lean forward and open the curtain hiding me from the hungry eyes outside. It's show time.

At first, I can't see anything in the relative darkness outside. Then I begin to sense movement and the shapes of bodies. Three men with shaved heads pass close by the window. They pause, leering at me. I run the thongs of the whip through my fingers and give them what I hope is a superior smile. Two of them look embarrassed and avert their eyes. The third licks his lips.

Then they're gone, and there's a new group, older, Teutonic-looking, with grizzled hair and thick mustaches. They huddle together, point at my toys, and laugh raucously. I rub my exposed, leather-covered crotch with the whip handle, before swishing the tails through the air. One of them raises his hand to the doorbell. I hold my breath. His companions stop him, point further down the lane. My window goes empty.

Damn. I'm so horny by this point that I'd be willing to screw a smelly German old enough to be my grandfather. That's what I think, anyway, until a beefy young man with a crew cut rings my bell.

"Good evening." I summon all my charm, but remain cautious. "Looking for some fun?"

"How much, Suzie Wong?" He leans close, trying to worm his way into my space. There's so much alcohol on his breath that I feel dizzy.

"Well, that depends on what you want." I back away, and narrow the gap between door and frame.

"I want to fuck your little chink cunt. How much?"

"I charge a hundred and fifty for the first half hour." He doesn't look like he's that flush. His sweatshirt is grimy and he's got a day-old beard. Still, I don't want to antagonize him by refusing him outright.

"A hundred fifty euros? For your skinny yellow ass? Forget it!" He glares at me, then spits on the sidewalk and strides away.

I sink back into my chair, shaking a bit. This isn't as easy as I thought it would be. I pick up the vibrator, turn it on, and hold it between my palms. The buzz travels through my body. My nipples tighten to points of pure pleasure. My clit throbs slowly in counterpoint to the rapid beat of the toy.

A new figure stops and stares. He looks like a college student: jeans and a corded jumper that shows off his nice body, long hair falling over a high forehead, gold-framed glasses, sensitive mouth. There's raw desire in his face. His hands are folded over his crotch; he can't hide the hard-on I know is there. I smile at him, encouraging, set the toy down on the table, and beckon to him. *Come in. I know what you need. I can give you what you want.*

He half-smiles, charmingly shy. *Please*, I silently beg him, *be brave. Ring the bell.* But he just stands there, watching me.

I scoop my breasts out of the corset and thumb the nipples. I have to close my eyes at the overwhelming sensation. He's still there when I open them again.

I cup my tits in my palms, offering them to him. My creamy skin is stained ruddy by the light. His lips part. I think that he will give in. Instead, he shakes his head, sadly, and walks out of the frame.

I slump in my chair, fuming. This is just a waste of my time and money. I slap the whip against my palm, relishing the sting, wanting to punish all the miserable creatures roaming the red-light district and ignoring me.

The bell rings. I throw the whip on the bed and open the door.

"Yes?" He's slender, forty-ish, with dark hair and a pale complexion. He's wearing a black turtleneck and a leather jacket.

"I want—I want to know about that." He points to the flogger. His hand is shaking. Lust races through my body like a fever.

"Would you like to come in and discuss it?"

"Ah … I'd like … how much do I have to pay?" He has an accent, maybe French. I get the feeling that he's as much a novice at this as I am.

"I'll charge you thirty euros." His look of relief confirms that this is within his budget.

"How long?"

"Until I say you can leave." For a moment I think that he will faint at these words, but then his somber face breaks into a weak smile. "Is that agreeable to you?"

"Yes. Yes, of course."

I open the door wider. "Well, get in here, then."

He slips into the cubicle, which immediately seems even tinier than before. I slide the curtains over the rod, shutting out the world, then turn to my first customer.

He's wedged between the bed and the wall, fists clenched, breathing hard. "Should I pay you now?"

"Later. Right now, I want you to strip."

He's awkward in the constrained space. "Hurry up. I want to see you naked."

"Yes, Mistress."

The unsolicited title sends a thrill through my body that settles in my cunt. Perhaps he's not as inexperienced as I thought. Or maybe it's just that he's played this scene out many times in his fantasies.

He's down to his undershorts when he hesitates. Sudden shyness? The stretchy cotton does nothing to hide the bulk of his hard-on.

"I said naked. Do I have to punish you for disobeying me?"

"No, Mistress. It's just …"

I pull out the waistband of his shorts and let the elastic snap back hard against his swollen cock. He shudders and gives a low moan. "No excuses." I yank the garment down to his ankles.

His cock springs out and bobs eagerly. The pleasingly curved shaft is as pale as his complexion. The bulging knob is fiery red. "That's better." I wish I could circle slowly around him, staring at his body until he blushes, but there's no room. In any case, I like what I see. His slender body has the strength of someone who walks a lot, not someone who spends hours in the gym. His chest is furred with dark curls, with a similar tangle at the root of his cock. Most of all, I like the expression on his face: desire and fear battling for supremacy.

I get the whip and dangle its thongs over his cock. His engorged flesh seems to swell further, to strain for more contact with the supple leather.

"So, you're interested in my little whip, are you?" I really don't know where this dialogue is coming from, but it feels right. "What would you like me to do with it?"

He stares down at his feet, where his undershorts are still tangled around his ankles. I suddenly have a clear sense of his emotions, confusion and shame struggling with lust. I understand how hard it must be, to admit a desire for humiliation, for pain.

"I asked you a question. If you don't answer me, I'll send you away."

"No, please, don't."

"Well then, what do you want? You're paying for this, after all."

He mumbles something incomprehensible.

"Speak up!" I snap the whip down on the bed for emphasis. His cock jumps.

"Beat me. Please, Mistress. Whip me." He looks me in the eye, his honesty frightening and arousing. "That's what I want. What I need."

Turning my back on him, I pick up the restraints from the table. His eyes widen.

"Kneel on the bed, with your back to me. No, leave the shorts on. They'll save me from having to bind your ankles."

In the confined space, encumbered by his underwear, he struggles to obey. His trials would be comic in some other situation, but at the moment they're an amazing turn-on. I'm generally pretty bossy, but I've never before had a man willing to comply with my every order. It's intoxicating.

His cock sways as he positions himself according to my directions. His thighs are lean and tanned, with a sprinkling of hair. The pale moons of his ass are completely hairless. I can see that the skin there is sensitive.

My cunt is overflowing. The thong is so soaked that it's beginning to chafe. I consider changing the scenario, flipping him over, straddling him, and riding that sweet, hard cock until I'm satisfied.

But that's not what he's paying for. Meanwhile that vulnerable, baby-soft ass of his is waking new and different desires in me. My cunt's on fire; I want to make his ass burn just as hotly.

"Lean forward, chest against the bed. You can turn your head to one side. Spread your legs. I want to see your balls dangle."

He almost loses his balance but manages to obey. "Good." I stroke his butt gently. My touch makes him shiver. "Now put your arms behind you—hands at the small of your back."

The restraints are leather, lined with soft felt and fastened with Velcro. I wrap one around each wrist, then clip them together. "Too tight?"

"No, Mistress."

"Tight enough? Try to move." He wriggles around, making his cock and balls vibrate appealingly. I lean over the bed so I can see his face. His eyes are half-closed; his lips are parted. "I have a feeling that you'd prefer tighter, more painful bonds, but this will have to do for tonight."

The whip handle feels surprisingly comfortable in my grip. I experiment, whisking the thongs through the air, trying to get a sense of the balance. Then I bring them down hard on the bed beside my victim. He jumps.

"Are you ready?"

"Yes, Mistress."

"Ready for me to whip your ass raw? To beat you so hard that you won't be able to sit down for a week? Are you ready to show me what a pain-slut you are, how much you can stand, in order to please your mistress?"

"Yes," he whimpers. "Yes, yes ..."

I swish the whip above my head and his ass twitches. I take a deep breath. Aiming at his right cheek, I slash the thongs across the pale flesh.

The stroke falls true. I feel the vibration of the impact in my hand. The sound of the leather connecting with his flesh sends a shock to my sex. It's followed a fraction of a second later by my victim's moan.

Parallel pink stripes bloom on his tender skin. They seem unbalanced. Tentatively, I swipe the whip across his left cheek. I'm rewarded by a whelp of agony and a new set of rosy marks. A perfect match.

I'm suddenly mainlining power. Everything snaps into focus with that second whip stroke. I see, with total clarity, the target for my next stroke, and the one after that. The whip feels like an extension of my body. No, that's not right, it's an extension of my mind. I imagine a lovely pattern of traces on his upper thighs, and they burst into being, accompanied by his cries of pain. He moans and screams, flinches, tries to cover his backside with his bound hands.

"No! Keep your hands out of the way! Unless you want me to stop. Have you had enough?"

I hear muffled sobs. At the same time, his cock is straining toward his belly, and his balls are tight and hard.

"No. More—please, give me more."

I paint his thighs, back, and butt with intricate designs in shades of red. He's close to coming and, oddly, so am I, though he hasn't touched me. I think that tomorrow, he'll examine my handiwork, feel the stinging memory, and come again. The notion pleases me, so I beat him faster and with greater force.

Finally, I have to rest. "More," he whimpers. He's drenched in sweat, hair tangled over his eyes. He's shivering.

His whole backside is crisscrossed with my marks. In some places, the welts blend together to form one raw, pulsing field of red. I graze a fingernail across one of these areas. He screams.

"No more of the whip. You've had enough. I told you that I'd decide when you should leave."

"No, please, let me stay ..." He tries to heave himself back up onto his knees. I push him back down.

"I didn't tell you to move. Be still. Let me look at you."

I can't believe I've done this to him. That he allowed me, begged me, to do it. Even more, I can't believe how the sight of his ravaged body turns me on. Maybe I should make him fuck me now?

But I mustn't let him know the effect he's had on me. I have to stay aloof in order to wield this power.

I can see his erection clearly through the V of his spread thighs. I can also see the brown dimple of his anus, safely hidden from my whip in the valley between his cheeks. I lean over and brush my fingers over the knot of muscle. He starts at the unexpected contact.

"You're unmarked, here." I wriggle my finger a bit, trying to work my way in. I can hardly breathe. I've never touched a man so intimately before. "It seems a shame." The flesh there is damp, taut, rubbery. Strange and infinitely exciting. "It's a pity. The tails of the whip can't reach you here. But I could always use the whip handle to fuck your asshole ..."

I push hard. My finger sinks in up to the first joint. He clenches around me, bucks, yells, spatters come all over the rented sheets.

I understand that it's not my finger that made him come. It's my words, my images. My mind, speaking to his. The physical power is just an echo.

He collapses on the bed. I let him lie there for a few minutes, to recover. I stroke his hair back from his forehead and tell him he's a good slave.

My sex is still heavy and aching with my own desire, but that somehow seems far away, much less important than I would have expected.

He's shy and grateful afterward. I sit in the armchair, watching him as he dresses. He's definitely a handsome man. When he pulls his wallet from his pocket and tries to give me a hundred euros, I shake my head.

"Thirty. That's what we agreed."

"But you gave me so much—just what I needed."

"Never mind. Business is business."

"Please."

"I said no. Are you going to start disobeying me?"

He smiles, puts most of the money away, and presses a ten and a twenty into my hand. "Thank you. Thank you so much." For a moment I think he's going to kiss me. I wish that he would. But that moment passes. He reaches for the door, squeezes past me in the crowded room, and is gone, into the night.

I lean back in my hired chair staring at the bills in my hand. I'm sweaty. My hair has come loose from the clip and is tangled down my back. My arms ache.

When I unlace my corset, my breasts tumble out, the nipples as hard and sensitive as ever. I unsnap the leather panties, drenched and stained from my juices. They make a sticky noise as I pull them away from my pussy. The ripe smell of cunt rises, mingling with the bitter scent of semen. I reach for the vibrator, conveniently located in the tiny room. The cool stainless steel cylinder slides deliciously into my swollen cleft. I flip the switch to high and writhe helplessly as the vibrations trigger one ragged, ecstatic climax after another.

Epiphanies? Revelations? I don't think he'll forget this night. As for me, I know that the memory of his red-streaked buttocks and tear-stained face, my power and his surrender, will fuel intense orgasms long into the future.

I still feel high as I lock my door behind me and step into the street. I'm naked under my coat. Every sensation is frighteningly acute. A random breeze plays in my damp, bare sex. The smell of spilled beer mingles with the tang of autumn leaves.

The alleys are still crowded. I hear snatches of conversation in a dozen languages, riffs of jazz and rock 'n' roll. I sense the beat of the men's hearts as they congregate around some red-lit rectangle of glass. A lithe male figure in a turtleneck brushes past me and my breath catches in my throat. Images flood my mind—images of pale, pliant flesh, offering itself to me.

It occurs to me, as I make my way back to my five-star hotel and my ordinary life, that perhaps I am the one who was marked this night.

THE QUEENING CHAIR

Kate Dominic

You don't have to be a queen to enjoy a queening chair. You do, however, need to have a retinue of lusty men available, ready and able to wear their tongues out on the queenly nether regions presented on the opened seat of the low stool beneath which each royal retainer will lie.

Max loves eating my pussy, but it will be a cold day in hell when he slides beneath a queening chair. We're both hard-core dominants with no interest in seeking out nonexistent submissive sides. Fortunately, by the time we met, we'd been in the BDSM scene long enough to have learned how to negotiate getting our sexual and emotional needs met. We go to BDSM play parties together, spend the evening topping other people in bondage and spanking scenes, then come home, compare notes, and fuck each other senseless.

Neither of us was comfortable with penetrative sex with others—at least, not yet. When I realized how much I really wanted to try a queening chair, though, he thought about it, then said that even though a tongue sure as hell could penetrate—we both knew *his* did!—to him, oral sex wasn't the same as fucking sex. He bought me the queening chair, invited three trusted male submissive friends from our group over to entertain me, and went off to play poker with his nonkinky buddies.

When Max had gone, I took my time getting ready. I'd programmed my MP3 player with a selection of slow and sexy songs, all sung by men with deep, rough voices. I shaved my pussy silky smooth. I piled my hair on my head in my favorite jeweled clip and slid into a deep, scented bubble bath. Then I leaned back on my bath pillow and let those crooning sandpapery voices glide over my skin while my pores opened.

It wasn't long before my hands were sliding through the warm, slippery bubbles, stroking my breasts and my belly, moving down between my open thighs until I was so horny I couldn't help wiggling my fingers into myself. With my thumb on my clit, my index finger in my pussy, and my middle finger up my ass, I masturbated until my skin was flushed and I was breathing hard. Finally, I was so close to coming I just lay there, my fingers motionless inside me, concentrating on the feel of the air moving in and out of my hypersensitized body as the bubbles popped around me.

But I had no intention of coming before I was seated on my queenly chair. By the time I climbed out of the tub and wrapped myself in a thick, thirsty towel, I was primed for an evening of talented male mouth-performance.

For the evening's festivities I'd chosen a black leather bustier, short gold velvet skirt, and thigh-high leather boots. As I finished styling my hair, I could hear my submissives arriving downstairs, greeting each other as they disrobed and set up the living room per the detailed directions I'd sent them during the week. I had no doubt that by the time I made my entrance they'd be naked except for their cock rings.

It's so lovely playing with well-trained submissives. When I walked in the room, the queening chair was in the center of the carpet—low to the floor, the well-oiled leather of the padded arms and back bar forming a C-shape around the opening in the middle. Below that opening, the cylindrical neck pillow hung from silver chains that gleamed in the firelight. I had no doubt it was already adjusted to position the mouth of the first of my servants at exactly the right height to service me. Next to the chair was an antique end table, covered in a pristine white linen cloth. On it rested a glass of sparkling water in a crystal goblet, a just-opened box of Godiva chocolates, the TV remote, the latest issue of *Cosmopolitan,* and my cell phone.

The only sound in the room was the crackling of the logs in the fireplace. I lifted my skirt just enough for it to clear the arms and back of the chair. Then I squatted down with my boots just outside the chair legs and adjusted myself until I was comfortable. It took me a minute. Although the chair supported my weight well, my knees were bent deeply. The position spread my pussy lips and my anal crack deliciously wide, though. I snapped my fingers, picked up my glass and the remote, and turned on the TV.

Those wonderful men had set the station on the Food Channel. A special on angel food cake was just beginning. I picked up a bonbon, biting into a juicy cherry truffle as the lusciously muscular and spectacularly hung Darin slid his head beneath my skirt. The women in our club considered him an Adonis, and he was a masochist to his core. He was usually naked in my presence—my submissive in many percussion scenes. I had never before allowed him access to my pussy.

He appeared determined to show himself worthy of the honor. His erection stretched above his belly button, the gleaming red head so stiff it had pulled completely free of its cover. His forehead bumped my thigh as he positioned his head on the pillow. He kissed the spot in apology. Then his hands gripped the chair legs and his hot, wet tongue slid like silk the entire length of my newly shaved slit.

I shivered so hard I almost dropped my glass. Max was no slouch at tonguing me to orgasm, but Darin was worshiping my pussy. With each tender, delicate swirl, my clit seemed to reach for his tongue. I drew in a deep breath, my hand shaking so badly I could barely set my glass back on the table. He swiped the full length again. I arched my back, pressing my pussy into his mouth as I imagined my exquisitely sensitive nub growing more engorged with each taste. I imagined it puffing and stretching out from under its tiny hood, displaying itself in a way that invited even more dedicated attention.

Darin rose to the task. As pre-come drooled from the long, deep slit at the tip of his penis, he flicked his tongue mercilessly over my clit. He wasn't even stopping to breathe, just ruthlessly flailing with a constant, steady friction that seared sensation beneath and over and around—and deep up into the exquisitely tender area that so rarely peeked out of its protective cover.

The orgasm stunned the air from my lungs. I screamed. Screamed again, thrusting my pussy down hard onto his face. He wrapped his lips around my clit and sucked. I shrieked and came again.

Even through my shaking, I could feel Darin's face sliding on my juices. When I finally leaned forward to rest, he went back to long, slow swipes up my slit, no doubt licking up the evidence of my orgasm before passing the tongue baton to his colleague.

With my hand still trembling, I picked up my cell phone and speed dialed Max. He answered with a gruff, "How's it going?"

"I have just had the most incredible orgasm of my life!" My breath was still unsteady. Darin's quick kiss to my clit was too unobtrusive to have been anything but respectfully polite, yet I was learning the nuances of his lips on my pussy enough to know he was smiling.

"Better than me?" Max was laughing. I didn't answer. When he asked again, his tone of voice was guarded. "Babe?"

"Darin," I shivered as Darin's tongue swiped again, "is highly motivated."

"And I'm not?!"

The stifled snicker from behind me told me that Max's ire was carrying across the room.

"You're not under a queening chair, tonguing my pussy to ecstasy."

As Max harrumphed into the phone, the tongue on my clit again started flicking. I moaned with pleasure.

"What's going on now?!"

"Darin is tonguing my clit again. You know how I like it—fast and steady, even though your tongue gets tired really fast. But he's not wearing out."

Darin's tongue had been slowing, but as I spoke, the speed picked up with renewed vigor. Over, under, around. Flick, flick, flick.

"Ooh! He's licking way up on top! You know—that special spot that's usually hidden under my clit hood." Darin took direction like a charm. "Right there. Don't stop! Oh, fuck, yes— DON'T STOP!"

I screamed as I came, right into the phone. Darin kept his tongue dead on, flailing his target as I bucked and howled and my pussy juice squirted onto his face.

"Oh, God!" I shuddered, pressing my pussy down onto his lips. "I just squirted!"

"No shit!" Max was laughing now. I had no doubt his pride was more than a tad bruised. But Max was a pragmatist. If something worked, it worked—and he was the first to admit it. "You're taking notes for me?"

"Of course." I had no doubt I'd have plenty of tips for him, when I finally quit coming. With my pussy once more humming, I lifted my left foot, touching the pointed leather toe to the tip of Darin's deep-red, jutting shaft. He groaned beneath me, his lips closing around my clit, sucking the tender little hood against the flesh beneath as I dragged my toe downward. Suddenly, he bucked beneath me, moaning against my skin as come spurted from his cockhead. I smiled as my pussy shuddered again.

"Darin is going to stop now, though." His lips immediately stilled. "He just came all over my boot. So he's going to clean it up. And he's going to rest his marvelous mouth so it can service me more, later. In the meanwhile, Richard is going to take his place beneath my queening chair. Richard will no doubt strive to live up to the precedent his colleague has set."

"I'm going to listen."

I didn't respond, just watched the neck and torso still trembling at the edge of my skirt. Darin kissed my pussy good-bye and slid out from under me. His handsome face was smeared with my juices and flushed a beautiful dark red. He looked thoroughly sated.

"Babe?"

I don't take orders from anyone, including my husband. I watched Darin wiping my shoe for a moment. "You were saying …?" I purred into the phone.

I could almost hear Max gritting his teeth. Finally he snapped out, "I was saying, I'd like to listen—sweetheart—while Richard eats your pussy." When I still didn't answer, he growled, "Please."

I smiled into the phone, waving Darin over to the couch for a well-earned break. "Of course—sweetheart. Richard's sliding into place now. I'm used to seeing his pretty, dark curls bobbing while I flog him. This will be quite a new experience, seeing only his legs and torso and his lovely, short, thick cock waving above him while he worships my pussy."

I gasped as Richard's tongue swiped slowly upward. His tongue was different than Darin's—short and stocky, like Richard overall. He licked sweetly up, circling my clit with the flat of his tongue until I was trembling. Then he moved slowly back down. Down. Parting deep between my labia—and sliding in. His tongue wasn't long enough to probe very far. But it was fat and hot and talented. I had no doubt he was going to play that magical first inch of pussy wall in ways I'd only dreamed of.

"Babe?"

"Wait, Richard." His tongue instantly stilled. "Max, I'm putting the phone on the table beside me. You may listen, but don't interrupt. Richard is going to tongue fuck me until I scream. I don't want any distractions."

I ignored Max's sputtering as I stretched arms high, reaching for the ceiling as I grinned and resituated myself on the chair again. I ate another bonbon, this one buttercream, and glanced at the TV long enough to see we'd now moved on to preparing a dinner party for twelve on twenty-four hours' notice. Definitely not something I'd be doing without the services of a talented waitstaff. By the time I'd taken another drink and set my glass down again, the sputtering in my cell phone had gone silent. But the light was still on. I knew Max too well to think for one minute that his voyeuristic streak wouldn't have his ear glued to the phone. Richard's breath teased lightly over my pussy lips.

"You may begin."

I'd always thought a long, agile tongue was a prerequisite for proper pussy eating. Richard's tongue was as short and stocky as the rest of him, and he was eating my pussy into fits. He started where Darin had left off, swirling the broad, flat top of his tongue over my clit until I was once again trembling above the mouth below me. But where Darin had used his supremely agile tongue to tease my engorged clit to poke up free of its hood, Richard licked and stimulated those overloaded synapses against the exquisitely sensitive nerves lining the inside of my hood.

Once more, I yelled when I came. But unlike when Darin had been licking directly on my clit shaft, this time I wasn't too overstimulated for continued friction as I came. Richard was able to continue the lovely, orgasm-inducing laving through every glorious wave.

When my trembling finally slowed, his hot, thick tongue licked slowly downward. He worshiped my outer labia, then the inner, working his way down my pussy. When he reached the opening where my pussy juice dripped out wet and slick, he licked until I was certain he'd lapped up every clear, tangy drop. Still licking, he slid his tongue inside.

My husband's tongue is talented. But no way was Max's tongue wide and stiff enough to emulate a short, thick dildo the way Richard's did. Once again, Richard used friction, pure and simple, to stimulate me. He was as tenacious as a bulldog, concentrating his entire being on that first magical, nerve-rich inch at the opening of my pussy.

He moved slowly at first, then faster and faster, then slowly again. I pressed down onto his face, panting and moaning as his tongue slid up and down around the inner walls of my pussy entrance. Then he started a slow, deep circling. His touch made me so hungry—hungry for tongue and cock inside me. Hungry for taste and smell and sensation. I pressed down harder, moaning as his tongue slid deeper. My breath was coming heavily. My nipples were pebbled hard against my bustier. I was *hungry!*

I plucked a bonbon from the box, sweat beading on my

breasts as I popped a dark round chocolate in my mouth. I bit. Cherry juice spurted across my taste buds as Richard's relentless tongue finally drove me over the edge again. Chocolate-flavored cherry juice slid down my throat as I tipped my head back, smiling and swallowing and groaning—pressing my pussy down onto Richard's face to keep his supremely talented tongue firmly inside me until I finally quit quaking.

I looked down at my lap, at the hairy chest sticking out from under the hem of my gold velvet skirt. Richard's stocky, drooling cock waved up toward his belly button. I lifted my legs, shivering as his tongue speared even deeper into me. His whole face was buried so far in my pussy lips I didn't know how he could breathe.

From the condition of his cock, I didn't think I was going to need long. I caught his shaft between the inner sides of my boots. He lifted his hips, moaning and fucking his tongue into me fast and furiously as my boots pumped him. Four, five, six times. Groaning loudly, he spurted all over my shoes—much the way Darin had, though I was stunned at the sheer quantity of semen coursing down Richard's shaft.

My boots were going to need some serious care, but I figured I'd send one home with each of them and, at our next group play party, flog the one who'd done the best job. I slowly lowered my feet to the floor and sighed.

"That was delicious, Richard. You may rest now." I picked up the phone, sighing as Richard tenderly kissed both sides of my pussy lips, then my clit, and slid free.

The green "active" light still glowed on my cell phone. "Max," I said, stretching languorously. "Are you still there?"

"Yeah," he growled. He sounded disgruntled, though not truly upset. "You were being awfully quiet there."

My husband was jealous! I smiled as I realized I was enjoying that. Not that Max really took our sex life for granted, but the heat had been fading a bit. We both liked spice. Sometimes hot, stinging spice. Maybe it was time to add a sprinkle of cayenne. Our relationship was solid. So was our communication. Max knew I was being serviced in my queening chair tonight. A bit of spice would make for some interesting negotiations later on.

"Richard's tongue is like a short, fat dildo," I purred. "It was exquisite."

Max growled into the phone. Richard blushed and inclined his head respectfully. I snapped my fingers at Carlos. His dark eyes glittered with mischief as he lowered himself and slid beneath me.

"I didn't know you liked dildos."

"Sexual innovation is always exciting. It keeps things from getting dull."

Max's breath exploded into the phone. "Are you saying our sex life is dull?!"

The little green monster was definitely biting Max's butt. I shivered as Carlos licked the insides of my thighs. Light kisses, then licks, moving slowly upward. Oh, yes—this man's tongue was long and agile!

"I've never tried a living dildo before. It was quite exceptional. Thick and stiff. Not deep, but wonderfully able to sense my responses and adjust position and rhythm accordingly. The constant friction made for an extraordinary orgasm. If Richard could bottle his tongue, he'd be quite rich."

I inhaled sharply as Carlos's tongue swiped hot and fast over my clit. Carlos had a reputation for being competitive. I had no doubt he would go out of his way to surpass both Darin and Richard—and to please me enough to really rile Max.

"You're breathing hard."

I smiled at my husband's waspish comment. Despite his

annoyance, his voice held the bossy timbre that said he was getting turned on.

"Carlos is licking my clit. His tongue feels like a living vibrator." I groaned and picked up another bonbon. Chocolate buttercream. My favorite. I let the sweetness slide over my tongue. "Mmm."

"Now what?!"

I gasped as Carlos's tongue lashed down my slit.

"What's going on?!"

"He's licking into my pussy." I groaned and Max sighed loudly. Carlos's tongue flicked in and out like a snake. "Ooh, he's talented!"

I froze as Carlos's tongue swiped further back.

"Babe?" Max caught the change in my breathing. "Are you okay?"

Carlos's tongue slipped lightly into my crack.

"Yes," I whispered. Carlos was laving the length of my crack. Touching. Tasting. Stroking the virgin skin. I'd been fucked in the ass before. But no one had ever worshiped me there. I gasped as his tongue swirled over my anus.

"Honey? Are you all right?" There was real concern in Max's voice now. "Answer me, dammit!"

"He's licking me," I whispered. "Back there." I licked my lips, searching for the words as Carlos's tongue washed over me in wide, slow circles. "He's licking my—anus."

Max's chuckle was low and sexy. "Do you usually like that?"

I stiffened as Carlos's tongue probed into the center. "I d-don't know," I panted. "Nobody's ever done it to me before."

Carlos's tongue stilled.

"No shit?" Max was laughing now. "I never knew that. Damn, honey. You're in for a real treat!" He paused. Then his voice got quiet. "Does Carlos know it's your first time? Make sure you tell him. He needs to know to make this really special for you."

Carlos kissed my anus. So sweetly and tenderly I couldn't help smiling. "He knows. Now."

Carlos was licking again. Washing again. Starting over. This time he was circling slowly from the outside in, then licking back out, long swipes from the center out to the edge, working his way carefully around my entire anal ring. I moaned in pleasure.

"Is he doing right by you?" Max's voice was back to normal—straight-forward, possessive, and determined to have me enjoy myself. "Lots of spit? Lots of foreplay?"

God, I loved that man. "Lots of spit and foreplay," I panted. "It feels really good!"

Carlos's tongue probed into the center again. This time, though, I was too relaxed to tighten.

"He's sticking his tongue—in my a-anus!" I moaned and dropped the phone. I could hear Max yelling, but what Carlos was doing felt too good for me to think about anything else. He was slowly working his tongue into me. I wasn't tightening. Not really. But I was too stunned to do anything but sit there and enjoy the feel of his tongue pressing in.

Suddenly, Darin was next to me, picking up the phone.

"Beg pardon, sir. Mistress can't talk right now ... Yes, sir. She's fine ... Yes, she definitely appears to be enjoying herself."

Enjoyment didn't begin to describe what I was feeling. The tip of Carlos's tongue was flat against me, then it pressed down and in. Hot flesh slipped between my anal lips. I groaned and thrust against him.

"Ma'am, sir says to bear down, like you're having a BM. If it pleases you do to so, ma'am."

I obeyed without thinking, bracing my feet against the floor.

I gasped as Carlos's tongue slid in deep. He kept it there, root-
ing around, slowly licking the sides of my anal ring. Getting me
used to the feel of his hot, wet tongue flesh fucking me. Fucking
my ass.

"Beg pardon, sir. I know you didn't say 'if it pleases you to do
so, ma'am.' But I have to say that, sir. I'm her submissive!"

I looked up to see Darin grinning at me, his eyes sparkling as
he held the phone far enough away from his ear to keep from
being deafened by the tirade of swearing issuing from it. I narrowed my eyes at him.

"Give me that phone. No—hold it by my mouth." Carlos
was sucking the side of my asslip. It felt so good I could hardly
breathe.

"Dammit, Max! Stay the fuck out of this! If you want to
listen, fine. But I don't want to hear one more word out of your
mouth unless it's to say something that's going to make me come
harder!"

Darin covered his mouth, hiding his snicker. Richard was beside me as well, though his head was turned and he was wiping
his lips. Carlos loosened his grip just enough to move up a bit.
Then he was sucking on the next section of my anal lips. I bore
down again, my groans getting louder as he took even more of
me between his rhythmically pulling lips.

"Yes, sir." Darin moved next to me, nodding as he dropped
to his knees. "By your leave, ma'am, when you're ready, your
husband wants me to suck your nipple. And he wants Richard
to finger your clit, so you get a really good come while your asshole's being licked." He held the phone out to me, but close to my
mouth, rather than my ear. "And he wants to listen, ma'am. When
you're coming. He said if he can listen to you come while your
asshole's being licked, he'll keep his big fucking mouth shut."

Darin's face was so close to the top of my bustier, I could feel his breath. But he didn't move closer. Richard's hand rested on the hem of my skirt, but he didn't lift it. "If it pleases you, ma'am. Your husband would like to hear you scream when you come."

Max was such an asshole. But I wouldn't deny either one of us sharing my virgin analingus orgasm. I nodded and reached beneath myself, gripping the edges of the chair. Darin moved the phone right up next to my lips. With his other hand, he opened the top of my bustier. He lifted my breasts free, then bent his head to my nipple. He licked as my hem lifted. Richard's fingers slid up my leg, dipping down in front, sliding onto my slick, swollen clit as Darin sucked my nipple into his mouth.

Carlos was licking in circles again, gentling my anus to relax, seducing it to open further.

"If it pleases you, ma'am." Darin's breath was hot on my wet, pebbled nipple. "Your husband suggests your bear down hard when Carlos really starts tongue fucking your asshole. He says that'll open you wide enough for him to get in really deep. He says it'll let you come so hard that you'll see stars." Carlos was probing again. Darin kissed, blowing softly just before he latched on again. "Your husband respectfully requests you come so hard your scream blows out the microphone on the fucking cell phone."

My laugh came out somewhere between a moan and a cry as Carlos's tongue once more pressed flat on my anal gate. This time, though, when he pressed in, I pressed out to meet him. His tongue slid in deep. Then it was out. And in. And out. I bore down hard, again, reaching for his tongue with my asshole as he once again slid in deep—and stayed. As I pressed against him, he licked the inner walls of my sphincter. Then he was tongue fucking me again.

The pressure was starting deep in my belly. Darin's talented lips on my nipple and Richard's equally talented fingers working my clit were beyond exquisite. But the orgasm was starting deep in my asshole. Starting where Carlos was fucking my asshole with his tongue. As the splendor raced up through my body, I screamed. "Don't stop! Please, don't stop! PLEASE!"

I wailed as the orgasm tore through me. Darin's lips were locked on my nipple, sucking hard as Richard's hand kept up its relentless pace. And Carlos's tongue—Carlos's perfect, angelic tongue, was buried deep in my asshole, wriggling but not pulling out as my spasming sphincter clamped down like a vise around him. Something hot and wet hit my leg. My asshole clenched so tight I was certain I'd push him out. But Carlos's tongue stayed deep, letting me glory in the ecstasy of my first true anal orgasm. When he finally pulled back and kissed my quivering anus, I was still shaking so hard, I almost fell off the chair.

I looked down at the torso beneath me. This time, I wasn't going to have to take my boots to the man beneath me. Carlos's chest and belly and Richard's arm and my leg were covered with glistening white puddles. A final line of semen dripped from the head of Carlos's now only half-hard cock.

I lost track of how many times I came—and how many times they changed places. Eventually, I told Max I'd talk to him when he got home. I hung up and watched a chick flick he hated and ate more bonbons and drank my sparkling water and even some champagne Darin brought me from the kitchen. I called my girl-friends. There's nothing in the world quite like sipping bubbly and watching movie stars with tight butts making slow, tender love to their women—all the while chatting up a play-by-play of the movie with my totally vanilla best friend from college. With each breath I took, an anonymous tongue beneath me worshiped my quivering pussy or my equally tingling anus.

Max got home shortly after I'd sent the others on their way. I fucked him so long and hard, I even wore him out—no mean feat for a man renowned for his stamina and horny beyond belief from listening to me come over the phone. He rolled me over on my tummy and slid his lube-slicked cock up my still hypersensitive ass. I screamed and came again, milking the juice from his cock as he grunted and growled and told me he loved me.

The next day, I was still so horny, I jumped his bones before he was even all the way awake. Max didn't get the reputation he has in the pussy department by being a slouch. He took me out to dinner in a classy restaurant, we renegotiated our sexual agreements, and by the next Friday night, he'd arranged for his three now wildly enthusiastic friends to join us again at the house.

This time, it was definitely going to be "us." Max still wasn't going to crawl beneath the queening chair. But he was going to feed me peeled grapes and tell me dirty stories and kiss me and suck my tits when I came. When he got too horny, he was going to jerk his dick, but he wasn't going to let himself come until after everyone else had gone home. Then he was going to fuck me in every orifice I wanted. No matter how many times I'd already climaxed that evening, he was going to pleasure me enough to be sure I came at least one more time—with him.

ABOUT THE AUTHORS

TARA ALTON has published stories and essays in numerous webzines such as Clean Sheets, Scarlet Letters, Mind Caviar, and Blue Food, and she has stories in the print anthologies *Best Lesbian Erotica 2006, Hot Women's Erotica, The Mammoth Book of Best New Erotica,* and *Best Women's Erotica.* Check out her website at www.taraalton.com.

LISETTE ASHTON is a U.K. author who has published more than two dozen erotic novels and countless short stories. Writing principally for Virgin's Nexus imprint, as well as occasionally writing for the CP label Chimera Publishing, her stories have been described by reviewers as "no-holds-barred naughtiness" and "good dirty fun."

KATHLEEN BRADEAN's stories can be found in *Amazons: Sexy Tales of Strong Women, Best of Best Women's Erotica, Cream,* and *Garden of the Perverse,* as well as the Clean Sheets and Erotica Readers & Writer's Association websites. Visit her blog at KathleenBradean.blogspot.com.

ADELAIDE CLARK likes to rough up her lovers and occasionally have them take their hand to her. She often makes them tell her every detail of their naughtiest fantasies, then endeavors to live them out. She's just getting started writing erotica, but she plans to pen many more dirty stories.

ANDREA DALE lives in Southern California within scent of the ocean. Her stories have appeared in *Best Lesbian Erotica,* Fishnetmag.com, *Ultimate Undies,* and *The MILF Anthology,* among others. Under the name Sophie Mouette, she and a coauthor saw the publication of their first novel, *Cat Scratch Fever,* in 2006 (Black Lace Books), and they have sold stories to *Sex on the Move, Sex in the Kitchen, Best Women's Erotica,* and more. In other incarnations, she is a published writer of fantasy and romance. Her website can be found at www.cyvarwydd.com.

KATE DOMINIC is the author of *Any 2 People, Kissing* (Down There Press, 2003), which was a finalist for a 2004 Foreword Magazine Book of the Year Award. Her most recent work is available in *Glamour Girls, The Best of Best Women's Erotica, Luscious, Naughty Spanking Stories from A to Z, First-Timers,* and *Garden of the Perverse.* Her column, "The Business End," appears monthly at the Erotica Readers & Writers Association (www.erotica-readers.com). She is a featured monthly writer at Lady Susan's "A Private Affair" (www.spanking-lifestyle.com). Check out her website at www.katedominic.com.

DEBRA HYDE avidly engages in many things sadomasochistic and stands particularly dedicated to her superior partner. Her fiction appears in many Cleis Press anthologies, the most recent of which are *Caught Looking: Erotic Tales of Voyeurs and Exhibitionists, Slave to Love: Sexy Tales of Erotic Restraint,* and *The Happy Birthday Book of Erotica.* Her S/M novel, *Inequities,* was published in 2006. Visit her at her blog, pursedlips.com.

NOELLE KEELY likes to think her writing has the very proper ancestor from whom she stole part of her pseudonym turning in his grave. Look for her work in *Red Scream* magazine. Under several other names, she is widely published in erotica and other genres. She has never played ottoman for a dom or domme, but has had a long career as "cat furniture," which is almost the same thing.

STAN KENT is a chameleon-hair-colored former nightclub-owning rocket scientist author of erotic novels who grew up in England and has a first-hand knowledge of the punishment handed out by sexy schoolteachers. He has penned nine original, unique, and very naughty works, including the *Shoe Leather* series. Selections from his books have been featured in the *Best of Erotic Writing* Blue Moon collections. Kent has hosted an erotic talk show night at Hustler Hollywood for the last five years. *The Los Angeles Times* described his monthly performances as "combination moderator and lion tamer." To see samples of his works and his latest hair colors, visit him at www.stankent.com or email him at stan@stankent.com.

N. T. MORLEY is the author of seventeen novels of erotic dominance and submission, most recently *The Dancer.* Morley's stories have also appeared in the *Naughty Stories from A to Z* series, the *Best New Erotica* series, and many other anthologies.

MINAROSE has been published previously in *Secret Slaves* and *Ultimate Undies*, both part of the Fetish Chest anthology series from Alyson Publications. She enjoys writing sexy stories of all types, but favors the realms of science fiction, fantasy, and all things supernatural. Also a freelance Web designer, she is always on the prowl for new and challenging projects. MinaRose lives, works, and plays in South Florida where the sun inspires her heated visions.

TERESA NOELLE ROBERTS has had erotica published (more is forthcoming) in the anthologies *Best Women's Erotica 2004* and *2005* (Cleis Press); *Garden of the Perverse: Fairy Tales for Twisted Adults* (Thunder's Mouth Press); *Secret Slaves: Erotic Stories of Bondage, The Sexiest Soles,* and *Ultimate Undies* (all three from Alyson Books); and many other anthologies, web-sites, and magazines. She also writes erotica with a coauthor as Sophie Mouette. Their first erotic novel, *Cat Scratch Fever,* was released by Black Lace Books in 2006.

LISABET SARAI, some half a dozen years ago, experienced a ser-endipitous fusion of her love of writing and her fascination with sex. Since then she has published three erotic novels, including *Raw Silk,* and coedited the anthology *Sacred Exchange,* a collec-tion of fiction that explores the spiritual aspects of BDSM rela-tionships. Her latest work, a highly praised collection of her short stories, titled *Fire,* was released in 2005 by Blue Moon Books, and her erotic-noir novel, *Exposure,* was published by Orion in 2006. Sarai also reviews erotic books and films for the Erotica Readers & Writers Association (www.erotica-readers.com) and Sliptongue.com. She lives in Southeast Asia with her husband and felines. For more information on her and her writing, visit Lisa-bet Sarai's Fantasy Factory (www.lisabetsarai.com).

DONNA GEORGE STOREY spent a few summers in college working as an administrative assistant in Washington, D.C., but never got more action from the men who run our nation than lust-filled stares. Her fiction has appeared in Clean Sheets, Scarlet Letters, *Taboo: Forbidden Fantasies for Couples, Foreign Affairs: Erotic Travel Tales, Garden of the Perverse: Fairy Tales for Twisted Adults, Sexiest Soles: Erotic Stories About Feet and Shoes, Mammoth Book of Best New Erotica 4* and *5, Best Women's Erotica 2005* and *2006,* and *Best American Erotica 2006.* Read more of her work at www.DonnaGeorgeStorey.com.

ALISON TYLER is the author of more than twenty explicit novels, including *Learning to Love It, Strictly Confidential, Sweet Thing, Sticky Fingers,* and *Something About Workmen* (all published by Black Lace); and *Rumors* and *Tiffany Twisted* (Cheek). She is the editor of *Heat Wave, Best Bondage Erotica volumes 1* and *2, The Merry XXXMas Book of Erotica, Luscious, Exposed, Happy Birthday Erotica,* and *Three-Way,* and the coeditor of *Caught Looking* with Rachel Kramer Bussel (all from Cleis Press); and the *Naughty Stories from A to Z* series, the *Down & Dirty* series, *Naked Erotica,* and *Juicy Erotica* (all from Pretty Things Press). Please visit www.prettythingspress.com.

SASKIA WALKER is a British author who has had erotic fiction published on both sides of the pond. You can find her work in over thirty anthologies, including *Best Women's Erotica 2006, Red Hot Erotica, Slave to Love, Secrets 15, The Mammoth Book of Best New Erotica 5,* and *Stirring Up a Storm.* Her longer work includes the novels *Along for the Ride* and *Double Dare.* Visit her at www.saskiawalker.co.uk.

KRISTINA WRIGHT has written erotic fiction for more than thirty anthologies, including *Ultimate Undies: Erotic Stories About Lingerie and Underwear, Secret Slaves: Erotic Stories of Bondage, Caught Looking: Erotic Tales of Voyeurs and Exhibitionists, Best Women's Erotica 2000* and *2007*, and four editions of the Lambda Literary Award–winning series *Best Lesbian Erotica*. For more information about her life and writing, visit www.kristinawright.com.

ABOUT THE EDITOR

RACHEL KRAMER BUSSEL is a prolific erotica writer, editor, journalist, and blogger. She serves as senior editor at *Penthouse Variations*, hosts the In the Flesh Erotic Reading Series, and wrote the popular Lusty Lady column for *The Village Voice*. Her books include *Naughty Spanking Stories from A to Z 1* and *2, First-Timers, Up All Night, Glamour-Girls: Femme/Femme Erotica, Ultimate Undies, Sexiest Soles: Erotic Stories About Feet and Shoes, Secret Slaves: Erotic Stories of Bondage, Second Skins, Caught Looking: Erotic Tales of Voyeurs and Exhibitionism*, and the companion volume to *She's on Top*, titled *He's on Top: Erotic Stories of Male Dominance and Female Submission*. Her writing has been published in over eighty anthologies, including *Best American Erotica 2004* and *2006*, as well as *AVN, Bust*, Cleansheets.com, *Diva, Girlfriends*, Mediabistro.com, *New York Post*, Oxygen.com, *Penthouse, Playgirl, Punk Planet, San Francisco Chronicle*, and *Zink*. Visit her at www.rachelkramerbussel.com.

Printed in the United States
By Bookmasters